The Night The Lights Went Out In Georgia

Jeremy GT Reuschling

DEDICATION

This book is dedicated to you. Thank you for taking a chance on me and buying my book. It's been a long road from start to finish but I hope you enjoy each turn of the page.

~ Jeremy

CONTENTS

ACKNOWLEDGMENTS

There are so many people I want to thank and mostly these are the people who have had such an impact on my life.

First and foremost to my wonderful family. My mom Marci, my dad Eric, and my sister Stephanie. We truly are a remarkably close knit family and one that I consider myself so blessed to have. To my mom and dad, you have given Stephanie and I the most amazing life and are the greatest parents we could have ever asked for. No matter when we acted up or screwed up you were always there for us and I can't thank you enough. I love you both from the bottom of my heart. And to you Stephanie, we were a typical brother and sister growing up and as the years went by our sibling connection only grew stronger. I'm so proud of everything you have done and love you so much.

To Dustin Soper. You have always been there for me through thick and thin. No matter if I needed you as a friend or to whip something up for me to use at work, you have always been willing to do whatever I asked you. Thank you so much for being such an amazing friend. Just please don't ever ask me to play 20 Questions again!

To Sara (Morrison) Carinder. The one person who I tell everything to, and I'm pretty sure you tell me almost everything. No matter if I have been on Cloud 9 or gone through the worst day of my life, I always know that you will be there for me. Thank you for being such an amazing friend and letting me raid your closet for treats!

To Bobby Burnette. You are such an amazing person and one that I couldn't be more proud of. I've told you this in the past and it's true. Because I saw your determination in pursing your dreams it gave me the motivation to finish this book and finally get it published. Thank you for everything and being a true friend!

To my own little posse. Jayna Friedrich, Joe Huebert, Taffy Nash, and Andrew Weaver. The stories I could tell about some of our get togethers! We have had so much fun hanging out through the years, and working together. I couldn't ask for a better group of people to call my friends.

To Kelley Hill and Jason Edwards. From the very first time we hung out together after the Royals game in Kansas City, to just hanging out and catching up on old times. You two are the craziest friends I have and cherish each memory we have created together. Isn't it amazing we've never gotten in trouble while being around each other?

To Lori Holliday. You gave me my first job and that's when I realized no matter how great of friends we may be, when it's time to work we work hard! Even if someone offers to break up the clumps of dirt for us to make our life so much easier you said no. I still haven't forgiven you for that to this day! You are such an important part of our family and you know we consider you one of us. Whenever we all hang out it's usually nothing but laughter and harassing each other.

To Nick Rehmus. It all started with a check and I'm so happy to say that we became such great friends. You always welcomed me and let me tag along wherever you were going. And thank you for everything that you did for me, no matter how cold or late it was.

To all of my grandparents, aunts, uncles, and cousins: Nessie & Damon Reeves, Arty & Dick Reuschling, Peggy Reeves, Pat Swain, Donna McMahon, John Reeves, Christina Braun, Jessica Esters, Megan Reeves, Brenna McMahon, Katie McMahon, Diana Summers, Ron Reuschling, Chris Summers, David Summers, and all of the rest of my extended family.

To Bobby Russell for writing such an amazing story telling song and to Vicki Lawrence who originally recorded the song that I remember my folks playing as a kid.

To Reba McEntire. You are my idol and all time favorite entertainer. You took this song and turned it into a country hit that you still perform live to this day! I love it. You are the reason why I decided to turn this song into a book. Especially after seeing the amazing video that you and Jack Cole had made. In my opinion it doesn't get any better than you! Thank you for always being someone that us fans could look up to.

To the following who have been a part of my life in one way or another and in no particular order. David Merida, Will Gausman, Brad Wooldridge, Katie Winningham, Linda Bruce, Christopher Graham, Jessica Dority, Wendy Yang, Betty Cramer, Theresa Young, Myrna Bruce, Melissa Hampton, LeAnn Shackelford, Jean Hampton, Susan Fortman, Christina Salyer, Nathan Cook, Andy Skelton, Lisa Williams, Karaunda Hurt, Bob & Jane Roach, Nichole Twenter, Shelby Brandes, Betty Brandes, Amy & Kevin Murdock, TJ Mitchell, Carlene Mitchell, Rob Thomas, Amy Imhoff, Annie Adair, Mandy Eichelberger, Logan & Jenny Espencheid, Wendy Wooldridge, Joel Gast, Tommy Larm, WJ's Staff, my Citizens Bank & Trust family, my Isle of Capri co-workers, German Alfonso-Amaya, Aubrey Sercu, Matt & Angie Shannon, Elizabeth Askren Tate, Jennifer Sandknop, Emily Voss, Isaac Bradley, Jim Dyke, Chris Carinder, Karen See, Travis Irwin, Lisa Felten, Kim Wolfe, Natlie Bartholomew, Rhonda Gibson, Carmen Wells, Michelle Vollmer, Spencer Miller, Caleb Forrest, Kathi & Frank Flagg, Laura Flagg, and anyone else I may have forgotten. Sorry about that!

1
MAKING THE DECISION

It was nearly 9:30 in the morning and the sun had already started to dry away the dew that rested on the blades of grass. A dark blue BMW slowly turns onto a gravel driveway kicking up rocks and dust behind it. The vehicle continues down the gravel drive and comes to rest at the first available parking spot.

The driver's side and passenger side doors open at the same time. Emerging from the vehicle are Kyle and Brooke, both of whom are in their forties. Kyle McAlister is a very tall, well-built gentleman. He practically lives every waking moment at the gym or the pool, which pisses his wife, Brooke, off to no end. Brooke is a very petite lady who used to work as a nurse. She quit her job three summers ago when Kyle's mom came to live with them.

Kyle and Brooke have had problems with their marriage for the past two years when it was discovered that Kyle had been cheating on his wife. He begged her not to leave him, and said how sorry he was, and how he wouldn't know how to live life without her. Going against all that she believed in, she took him back. But with him spending so much time at the gym, she often wondered if he was doing it for health reasons or if it was to impress somebody new.

Once Brooke shut her car door she opened the back passenger door to help an elderly lady out of the car. With one hand grasped firmly on her arm, Brooke helps out of the car her mother-in-law, Sarah McAlister. Sarah slowly gets out of the car, with her cane on her right side of her body using it as support.

"Here Mom, let me help you," Kyle said as we walked around the back end of the car.

"I don't need any of your help, Brooke is doing just fine. If it isn't too much to ask, please grab the flowers out of the back of the car," Sarah asked of her son in a sarcastic tone.

Sarah had come to live with her son and daughter-in-law several summers ago, just after Sarah had lost her husband. They had two children, Kyle and Bectel. Kyle was the older of the two born in 1957 and Bectel in 1959. Unfortunately Bectel never made it to his first birthday. Sarah had gone in to check on her newborn one morning and found that he had died in his sleep. There was never a cause of death determined, but some would speculate it would be today's "Sudden Infant Death Syndrome."

Kyle and Sarah were always very close, and she had looked forward to moving in with him and Brooke. And for Brooke being her daughter-in-law, Sarah treated her as if she were her own flesh and blood. However, Sarah's feelings toward her son changed when she had heard of the affair that had taken place. She still loved her son, but every now and then when she would get to thinking about it she would become upset, especially when it came to this time of year. On more than one occasion Sarah had told Brooke that she should leave him. Once a cheater always a cheater was how Sarah looked at it. After all it was an affair that had caused her parents to divorce, and her brother's death all those years ago.

That's why they were here. The three had gone out to the cemetery just outside of Sumertown, Georgia to put flowers out on the grave of Sarah's brother. All three of them walked quietly along a stone path that circled the cemetery. Once they got to the statue of Jesus with his arms spread apart, they stepped onto the wet grass and carefully walked along the rows of headstones. It took them awhile, as they had to go slowly because of Sarah's age and arthritis of the knees. After going a short distance, the three of them stopped. In front of them was a three-foot gray head stone. Engraved on it was:

"Raymond P. Turner

May 17, 1921-June 2, 1953

A beloved brother."

"You know, white roses were always his favorite," Sarah said while holding the roses under one arm. "He was a good man, and if it wasn't for that woman, he would still be here today," Sarah said aloud as her eyes began to fill with tears. She carefully bent down, using her cane for support. In the vase next to his headstone she placed a dozen white roses and slowly stood back up. Kyle then opened a bottle of Avian and filled the vase three quarters full of water.

"Mom, we need to get going," Kyle said as he began to walk away. Brooke grabbed Sarah by the arm, and with a little tug helped Sarah back to the car.

The mile drive back to Sumertown was a drive that Sarah hated. It was along this one-mile strip of road that it all happened so many years ago. As they came around a curve Sarah stared at the sign that read, "Welcome To Sumertown, Georgia ~ A Peach of a Town. Population 2723." Sumertown was a small but friendly town. It was the type of town where everybody knows everybody and their business, and people pass the time with gossip.

3

When one drives down Main Street, they are able to see everything. When you first get into town there is a Mom and Pop Shop with four gas pumps. A little bit further down is the courthouse, and at the very end of town is an old run down bar that was closed in the early 80's called Web's. Now, Web's was a happening place. John Maxwell had first started it in 1947. In fact, it was the one business that had been the most successful in its day. Every Friday and Saturday night the place would be packed with friends and family. And it was tradition that all wedding receptions would be held there. It stayed open until 1983 when John suffered from a massive stroke and died. John's family had no interest in keeping the place open, so it just sat there empty. There was always talk at the monthly town hall meetings of re-opening Web's, but with all the health regulations and codes that were now in place, it never actually happened. All it stood for now were memories for those old enough to remember.

Kyle and Brooke lived just outside the east end of town. They were among the wealthiest people in town, as Kyle and Brooke had both inherited a large sum of money when both of their fathers died. Brooke's dad was the judge for Sumertown from 1954 until the day he died in 1987.

Kyle's dad, Tim, and Sarah had their own business. Tim was a carpenter and had made most of the furniture that the people had either in their homes or businesses, and Sarah handled all their finances. Tim had started the business in 1956, and Sarah joined him after they got married in 1958. When Kyle was old enough, he then joined the family business and helped his mom and dad.

Kyle had gone away to law school, as his dream had always been to be a lawyer. It was during law school that he met Brooke. After his dad died, Kyle sold the business and made a large profit from it. By this point, Sarah was already very well set. She was upset that he had sold the family business but figured that it was for the best since he was always wrapped up with some trial. Besides, Sarah knew that's where his heart was.

Kyle and Brooke had built a large two story, 6 bedroom, 3-bath house that sat on 7 acres of land. They were famous for the large parties and barbecues they would host during the summer. As Kyle pulled into the drive, he let Brooke and Sarah off at the front and drove around to the side to park his car.

"These knees just aren't what they used to be, and that damn hip replacement surgery was a waist of my time!" Sarah said to Brooke as she climbed the stairs to the front door.

"Sarah, do you know how much I love you?" Brooke asked as she chuckled. Brooke unlocked and opened the front door and helped Sarah into the family room and onto the couch. As Sarah finally got seated she let out a sigh.

"Do you want me to get you some coffee?" Brooke asked.

"That would be wonderful dear. And spice it up a little, would you please?" Sarah asked. With a nod of the head Brooke turned around and walked through the arch opening into the dining room, and then into the kitchen. Brooke got a pot of coffee started, and got out three coffee mugs, cream, sugar, and Irish whiskey. Every once and awhile when Sarah's joints would bother her, she would put whiskey in her coffee to help ease the pain. She always said it was cheaper and more fun than going to the doctor. Kyle always disapproved of this, but never did anything to stop it. While waiting for the coffee to finish, Brooke began to make up some of her famous lemonade for the barbecue that they were going to have later that evening.

Kyle came in through the back, walked through the dining room, into the living room and to the front door. He opened the door and found his newspaper just a few steps down. He went down, picked it up, and then went back inside. Once inside, he went back into the living room and sat down in his leather chair. Brooke walked into the living room carrying a tray with three mugs on it. She handed one to Sarah, one to Kyle, and then sat down on the couch next to Sarah and had the last mug for herself. As she sat down, she placed the tray on the coffee table in front of her and looked over at Sarah.

"Is everything okay Sarah?" Brooke asked as she put her hand on Sarah's shoulder. Sarah just sat there holding her cup of coffee, staring off into the distance.

"Mom? Mom, Brooke asked you a question."

"Oh, I'm sorry. You know what, I think that I'm just going to take my coffee back to my room, do some reading, and take a short nap," Sarah said. With that she proceeded to get up.

"Here, let me help you honey," Brooke said as she got up with her.

"No sit, I'm all right," Sarah said as she started to walk around the front of the couch. "Wake me for lunch Kyle?"

"Sure Mom, if you need anything just holler."

With that Sarah walked across the living room back towards the front door, and went into her room. Her room used to be upstairs with everybody else. But after her hip replacement surgery, Kyle moved his office upstairs and his mom's room downstairs.

Kyle put his cup of coffee down on the floor, got up from his chair and grabbed a baby monitor from the dining room and turned it on. Kyle had put a baby monitor in his mom's room ever since she first moved in with them. If she ever needed anything or was in trouble they would know. He walked back over to his chair, sat down, and began to read his paper.

"Is she going to be okay?" Brooke asked.

"You know how she gets. This is a hard time for her. She was very close to her brother, they were around each other all the time. So, when he died, it was like she lost her best friend, even though he did kill that one guy. Just give her a day or two, and she'll be fine."

"I hope you're right. It just seems that with each passing year it gets harder and harder for her," Brooke replied as she took a sip of her coffee.

Sarah opened the door to her bedroom, walked over to her nightstand and placed her cup of coffee on the table next to the baby monitor. She then sat down on the bed and let out a sigh. Then ever so quietly she picked up the baby monitor and switched it off. She hated that damn thing. It made her feel like a child and prisoner all wrapped up in a small package. Sarah was always a very independent woman, and felt that anything a man could do, she could do ten times better. She turned it off all the time. Kyle never heard the click usually because he was busy doing something.

Sarah got back out of bed and went over to her closet. She opened the door to and pulled down on the chain that was suspended from the ceiling to turn the light on. On the second shelf was a very old shoebox that was covered in tape. Kyle always tried to get her to put all that, "crap," as he called it in a new box, but Sarah refused. "Why get something new when you can fix what you've got?" She would always ask him. She pulled the shoebox from the shelf, walked back over to her bed, sat down, and carefully pulled the top of the box off.

Inside the box were newspaper clippings, and lots of them, all of which were about her brother. There were articles that were written on how he had killed a man for sleeping with his wife, was found guilty, and sentenced to death immediately. Some of the articles even went as far as to talk about the bad marriage he was in, and how when he returned from Candletop, his wife had skipped town. As Sarah was reading the articles that talked about her brother, the affair that happened, the trial, and the sentencing, she began to cry. For too many years she had been keeping a secret, and it was eating her up inside.

She put all the clippings back into the shoebox, put it back in the closet, turned the light off and shut the door. She began to walk back over to her bed, and felt her chest start to get tight. She sat down on the bed, and picked up her coffee. As she was bringing it up to her lips, her arm began to shake. In a split second, Sarah dropped her coffee mug, which shattered when it hit the wood floor, and fell forward onto the floor as well.

"Did you hear that?" Brooke asked as she quickly turned her head around towards the direction of Sarah's room.

"Hear what?"

"I don't know, but I think it came from your mom's room."

"It couldn't have, we would have heard it," Kyle said as he pointed to the baby monitor. He stopped and listened, and then noticed that he didn't hear anything. Kyle always had it turned up pretty loud so that he could hear his mom breathing, especially at night. This time, he heard nothing. He jumped from his chair, ran across the room and stopped at his mom's door.

"Mom?" Kyle asked as he lightly tapped on the door. "MOM!" he yelled. With still no response he opened the door and found his mom lying face down on the floor. "Shit, Brooke call Dr. Robinson. Tell him there's something wrong with Mom."

Brooke ran over to the phone while Kyle picked his mom up off the floor and laid her down on the bed. "Mom, please don't do this to me," Kyle begged. He ran to the hall closet and grabbed a washcloth and began to wipe blood from her face.

"Dr. Robinson is on his way over," Brooke said as she came into the room. "Oh my God, Sarah," she said bringing her hand up over her mouth.

Within minutes, Dr. James Robinson had arrived at the house. He was an elderly man in his seventies. He was familiar with Sarah's health condition, and was sure that she had suffered from a heart attack.

"Kyle, I think your mom has suffered another heart attack. I need you to help me get her into my station wagon and get her over to the school." With a nod of his head they carefully but quickly carried Sarah down the stairs of the house and laid her down in the back seat of the station wagon. Kyle sat in the back with his mom, her head resting on his lap. Brooke followed out behind and got into the passenger side beside Dr. Robinson.

The station wagon peeled out of their driveway. They headed to the school, which was the only place the helicopter could land. Sumertown's hospital had long since closed since the population of the town wasn't nearly high enough to justify the cost of keeping it open. While on the way to the school, Dr. Robinson had phoned his emergency contact at Atlanta Memorial Hospital and requested a helicopter be sent over immediately.

By the time they got to the school's track, they could see off in the distance the helicopter coming. Luckily there was no one on the football field which was the only place the helicopter could land. It was now almost noon, and usually the football players were out there practicing. But today they had been sent home early due to the high heat index.

The station wagon parked on the track that circled the field as the helicopter came in for a landing. Once it landed, two E.M.T's came out the back end with a stretcher running towards the station wagon. "I'm sure she's had a heart attack. I don't know how severe, but it doesn't look good," Dr. Robinson told one of the E.M.T.'s. Once they got Sarah onto the stretcher they rushed back to the helicopter.

"We want to go with you," Kyle yelled over the roar of helicopter blades spinning overhead.

"Can't do both, only one of you," one of the E.M.T.'s said. Kyle got into the helicopter with his mom.

"I'll meet you there," Brooke yelled to Kyle. Kyle nodded his head as the EMT shut the door to the helicopter as it began to lift in to the air.

The flight to the hospital took only fifteen minutes, but to Kyle it seemed like a couple of hours. He felt helpless sitting in the back of the helicopter. All he could see was his mom's legs. There was an E.M.T. on both sides of his mom. They were hunched over what looked to Kyle as a lifeless body, working on her. He couldn't believe what he was seeing. He wasn't ready to let go, he wasn't ready to say goodbye.

At the hospital, Kyle sat in the emergency room waiting area. He had been sitting there for almost an hour, and no one had come to speak with him. He was also beginning to worry about Brooke. She should have been there by now. He knew that she wasn't good with directions, and with the confusion of everything, she probably forgot to grab the cell phone. He figured that it was worth a try. So Kyle got up out of the chair and walked across the room to the pay phone. He noticed a young woman sitting on one of the couches with her two young children. It was obvious that she had been crying. She sat there with each kid on either side of her with her arms around them saying, "Daddy's going to be okay. Daddy's going to be just fine. Jesus won't let nothing happen to Daddy." The children didn't understand as they were both very young. They were more interested in watching Sponge Bob Square Pants on TV. Seeing those kids made Kyle wonder why it was that he and Brooke had never decided on having any children of their own. They were always in their house. Brooke had three sisters and two brothers, so they always had nieces and nephews at their house on the weekends.

Kyle got to the phone and deposited fifty cents and dialed Brooke's cell phone number. After four rings he heard, "Hi this is Brooke. Sorry I mis..." He just hung up the phone.

Kyle walked back over to his seat feeling completely stressed and useless. He had a million thoughts racing through his mind. Was mom alright? Why hadn't anybody come to talk to him? What if she has already died and they just don't know how to tell him? No, that can't be it. They know how to tell a family this, they do it every day. What about Brooke? Is she lost? Why the hell hadn't anybody come out to talk to him, and what is keeping Brooke?

He rested his elbows on his knees and let his head fall into his hands. He just shook his head back and forth.

"KYLE!"

"Brooke, Christ, I was so worried about you. Are you okay?" Kyle asked as he ran up to Brooke and threw his arms around her.

"I'm fine, how's your mom?"

11

"I don't know. Nobody has come out to talk to me yet."

The two of them walked over to one of the vacant couches and just sat there. Kyle had his right arm around Brooke. All they could do now was wait.

It was now almost five o'clock and the emergency room had started to get busy. The heat had brought on a lot of the problems with the people.

"McAlister family?" A young gentleman had walked into the waiting area dressed in green scrubs and holding a flip chart. Brooke and Kyle had gotten up off the couch and started to walk towards the nurse. "Mr. and Mrs. McAlister?"

"Yes," Kyle replied.

"Great, if I could just get you two to follow me." With that the male nurse turned around and walked out of the waiting area. Brooke and Kyle followed closely behind him. They went down a long hallway. There was nothing there. No offices, no doorways, no pictures on the wall. They turned a corner where they saw several rooms. To the left of each of the rooms was a plaque that read "Waiting Room #..." and then each had its own number. The male nurse had led them into the fourth waiting room.

"If you folks would like to have a seat, Dr. Stewards will be right with you. Can I get you all anything?"

"No, we're fine," Brooke responded. With that the male nurse gave a slight nod and left the room, shutting the door on his way out.

Brooke and Kyle sat in the room without saying a word. What do you say at a moment like this? Kyle just looked about the room. They were sitting at a round table with four chairs surrounding it. There was a clock and two pictures hanging up on the walls which was painted a really ugly blue. Brooke just sat there with her head resting on the table.

There was a knock on the door as it began to open. Both Brooke and Kyle sat up straight, as a tall slender male in his thirties walked into the room.

"Mr. and Mrs. McAlister, my name is Dr. Stewards. First allow me to apologize for having you both wait so long, but we were wanting to get your mom stabilized and into ICU as soon as possible."

"How is she?" Kyle asked.

"I'm afraid she's not doing well," Dr. Stewards said in a sympathetic tone.

With that, Kyle and Brooke began to well up. Kyle reached over and put his hand around Brooke's.

"While we had her in the ER she coded on us twice. We ran an ECG and did determine that she has in fact suffered a massive heart attack. Her coronary arteries are nearly 80% blocked, and I'm afraid if we take her into surgery to try a stint that she won't survive. I'm sorry to tell you all this, but the best thing we can do is make her last few days as comfortable as possible."

"You mean...." Kyle asked with a large lump in this throat.

"She's lived a long life, I'm afraid there is nothing more that we can do for her now. I would suggest that you go ahead and call in her family."

Kyle and Brooke both lost it. They didn't want to accept what the doctor was telling them. They felt like they had been betrayed. He wasn't trying hard enough, they thought to themselves, he's just being selfish.

"Can we see her?" Brooke asked through her tears.

"Sure." With that, the three of them got up and went to the closest elevator. Once inside, Dr. Stewards pushed the "4" button which lit up. Once the doors to the elevator opened, Kyle and Brooke saw a sign in front of them that said, ICU to the left, waiting room to the right. Dr. Stewards went left down the hall, and Brooke and Kyle followed.

Once through the doors into the ICU they were led to the very last room in the back. There laid Sarah with monitors and IV's hooked up to her.

"If you need me or anything at all, just let one of the nurses know," Dr. Stewards told them. "I'll be back after awhile to see how things are going." With that he left the room.

Kyle went right up to his mom and gave her a kiss on her forehead. "Hey Mom, Brooke and I are both here."

"Kyle, is that you?" Sarah asked in a weak voice.

"Yeah Mom, it's me. How are you feeling? Do you need anything?"

"I'm just really tired and my chest is in a lot pain. Was that the doctor I just heard? What did he say?" With that, both Brooke and Kyle began to cry again. "What is it?"

"Just lay back and rest," Kyle told his mom.

"Kyle, please just tell me. I can take it."

"Mom, just lay…"

"Kyle don't make me ask you again." Sarah's heart monitor began to increase with the excitement. She didn't like it when people would hide something from her, especially if it was serious.

"They're not giving you long mom. A few days, maybe more, maybe less." Kyle whimpered. "Now is there anything that I can do for you?"

"Yes, yes there is. Brooke, honey grab that pen and paper off the food tray and write some stuff down for me please?" Sarah asked pointing towards the window where the food tray was located.

Brooke swallowed back the lump in her throat. "Sure Sarah." She walked over to the tray and picked up a pad of hospital paper and pen. She also pulled a Kleenex out of the box that was also on the tray and wiped her eyes dry. "Okay, I'm ready."

"Brooke, Kyle, I have been keeping a huge secret from everybody for over fifty years. And if the doctors are right, I need to clear my conscience before I die."

"Mom, what's going on?" Kyle asked. He was beginning to worry. What was it that his mom had done, and why was it such a huge secret?

"Look, I'm not going to tell anybody anything until I have everything I need, and everybody that I want here. Now Brooke, from the house I need several things. In my closet is an old shoebox, it's on the second shelf. Bring me that. Also need that old photo album with the pictures of me and Raymond."

"Okay," Brooke said as she continued to write.

"Kyle, I want you to get a reporter, preferably Bobby. He's such a good kid with so much potential. I also need you to get Josh. Have them all meet here at 9 o'clock," Sarah said.

"Mom, why do you need all of these people here?"

"Please just do as I ask," Sarah responded in her frail voice.

"Okay, we'll get everything for you," Kyle said as he rested his hand on top of his mom's. "Is there anything else?"

"No, that's all."

"Maybe it would be best for you to get some sleep," Brooke recommended.

"I think you're right. I'm just so tired," Sarah replied as she shut her eyes.

Both Kyle and Brooke got up from their chairs by Sarah's bed and walked right outside of her room.

"What do you think she wants to tell us?" Brooke asked Kyle with a puzzled look.

"I haven't got the foggiest."

"Well, I think that I'm going to go ahead and go home and get Sarah these things. I'm going to pack some clothes since we may be here for a while. I'll be back first thing in the morning."

"Okay, be careful going home," Kyle said as he hugged and kissed his wife goodbye.

Brooke left the room, and Kyle went to the ICU waiting room and began making his phone calls. Once he finished, he went back into his mom's room, pulled up a chair and stayed by his mom's side for the rest of the night.

2
WHAT WILL THEY THINK?

Kyle had gone through much of the night in a light sleep. He was constantly waking up every few minutes it seemed to make sure that everything was okay with Sarah. It was now coming up on seven o'clock the next morning, and Kyle was again in one of his light sleeps. Sarah had been awake for ten minutes now, and all she could do was stare at the clock. In only two more hours it would all start again. What would happen once she told everybody? Could they put her in jail? Would they do the same thing to her as was done to her brother?

These thoughts were running in circles around Sarah's head. Sarah lightly closed her eyes. "GET OUT OF HERE!" She'd had a flash back and saw her brother. Her heart rate was again beginning to pick up some. She took in a long deep breath, and slowly let it back out again. Sarah looked over at Kyle and saw that he was beginning to wake up.

"Good morning sleepy head," Sarah said to Kyle as she ran her fingers through his hair.

"Hey Mom, how are you doing?"

"I'll be better once this is all over with."

"Mom, I really wish that you would tell me what is going on."

"Kyle, I would much rather wait until everybody gets here. I don't think that I can go through with telling this story twice. Just remember that no matter what, I always have, and always will love you."

"Mom, you are really starting to worry me."

"There is nothing for you to worry about. This is all my problem, and I am going to need to deal with it in my own way."

With that, a silence filled the room. Sarah started to worry more and more with each passing minute. A million times she thought of calling it off. Maybe some secrets are just meant to be taken to the grave. Sarah looked about the room in which she was confined to, the one it appeared she could die in. Was it really her time to go? Was she ready to go?

"Good morning," Dr. Stewards said as he entered the room. "Well Sarah, I must say, somebody must be watching over you."

"Why's that?" asked Kyle.

"Well, your mom showed some great signs of improvement last night. I think that it is pretty safe to say that for now we may be in the clear," Dr. Stewards answered while taking Sarah's blood pressure.

"I still have a sharp pain in my chest," Sarah said as Dr. Stewards put an ear thermometer in her ear.

"98.6, very good. It's going to feel that way for a little bit. This one was more severe than your last two heart attacks. Also, you need to keep in mind that we did need to use the crash cart on you twice in the ER. What we need to do right now is make sure you get plenty of rest. I've got more rounds to do, but I'll be back in to check on you later on this afternoon."

"Thanks doc, I appreciate it," Kyle said as he shook Dr. Steward's hand.

"Well Mom, it looks like you've surprised us again. So, do you still want to talk to all those people?" Kyle asked looking down at his mom.

What could she say? It she didn't talk to them, the guilt would continue to eat away at her. If she did tell them, the consequence of her actions could be severe.

"Mom, what do you want to do?"

"I said that I had something to say, and I will not go back on my word," Sarah said staring straight ahead. She was dazed now, and had begun to break out in a light sweat. She was in her own little world, lost between thoughts. She knew how great it would feel to get such a huge burden off her chest, but never in her life had she been so afraid.

"Well, well, well, look who is doing much better this morning," Brooke said as she walked into the room. She was carrying a medium size box with the flaps folded in. "Here you go Sarah, everything on the list. I guess that it wasn't really too hard, since there were only two things that you needed." Brooke said as she chuckled. Brooke laid down a sack at the foot of Sarah's bed, which contained some personal items that Brooke thought she might need along with the items Sarah had asked for. "Morning baby," Brooke said to Kyle as she bent down to give him a kiss on the lips.

"Hey," Kyle responded. He knew the time was now close and couldn't begin to think of what was to come.

"Has the doctor been to see you yet, Sarah?" Brooke asked.

"Yes, he was just in here. Now there is a chance I could go through with the surgery."

"Great! As soon as you get home, you've got to make some of your famous peach cobbler," Brooke said. She looked down at her husband and was about to ask him what was wrong when there was a knock at the door.

"I'm sorry to interrupt, but there are some gentlemen in the waiting room that are here to see Ms. McAlister. They say that they aren't family, but that they were sent for," said a nurse standing at the door.

"It's quite alright, would you please have them come in?" Sarah said to the nurse as she sat upright a little. The nurse nodded and turned around and left. Sarah sank her head back down onto her pillow. She again let out another sigh. Her heart was racing now, and Brooke had noticed it on her heart monitor.

"Sarah, honey, calm down. Is everything okay?" Brooke asked in a concerned voice.

"I just want this to all be over with. And in a short while, it will be," Sarah responded.

Brooke looked over at her husband as if for an answer, Kyle just shook his head as if to say, I don't know.

There was another knock on the door. This time there stood two gentlemen, one very well dressed, and the other in his every day street clothes.

"Please, come in," Sarah said waving them in with her right hand, which was now shaking with fear. "Kyle, sweetie, would you see about getting some more chairs?" Sarah asked.

"Sure Mom."

"Bobby Maxwell, come over here and give me a hug," Sarah said reaching out her good arm. Bobby Maxwell was just a young twenty-year-old kid that would do odd jobs for Sumertown's paper, which was only published once a week. He was trying to get into the big times as a reporter, with a long-term goal of working for Dateline or 20/20. Bobby was the grandson of John Maxwell, the owner of Web's. Bobby was a jokester in school, and never really took things seriously. He came to the hospital in dirty tennis shoes, old faded jeans that had holes in the knee area, and a button up farm shirt.

"Hi Grandma Sarah," Bobby said coming up to her. He gave her a light hug and kiss on the cheek. Sarah was known as Grandma Sarah to many people in the town. People that ranged in age from two all the way up to their thirties. Sarah would baby-sit during the evenings and weekends when she and Tim weren't in the shop. She practically raised all of the kids in town. Sarah patted Bobby on the back and then pinched his ear.

"Oww," Bobby yelped. "Why'd you have to go and do that for?"

"Look at yourself Bobby, you're a disgrace. You come for an interview and this is how you show up? Boy I'm telling you, I suggest that you clean up your act, or you'll never get out of this town and into the big times. Why don't you use some of those brains helping you to dress, and not always onto the paper you write?" Sarah scolded. "But you know that your Grandma Sarah loves you no matter what."

"Yes Ma'am," Bobby replied rubbing his hear. By this time, Kyle had come back into the room with two fold up chairs. He handed one to Bobby, and set the other one up on the other side of Sarah's bed.

"Sarah, it's been a long time," an elderly man said coming up to her bed. His name was Josh Higsbey, and he had been the McAlister's family lawyer for nearly thirty years. He had gotten Kyle out of a lot of messes when Kyle had first started practicing law, and had made some bad choices. He was always dressed in his Sunday best. Well polished shoes, clean suit, and always a tie. Even if he were at a picnic, he would always have on a tie.

"It has been a long time Josh," Sarah said as she gave him a hug. Her voice was starting to sound tired now. "How've you and Lori been doing?"

"Fine, fine. She keeps telling me I need to go on a diet," Josh said as he put his hand on his potbelly. "But other than that, just been keeping busy. What about you, what's so important that you need two lawyers here?" Josh laughed pointing his thumb at Kyle. Everyone in the room chuckled, everyone except Sarah.

The room fell silent once they knew that Sarah hadn't found the poor attempt at a joke funny. She laid there for a moment, eyes closed, thinking. She kept having flash backs of her brother yelling at her, "GET OUT OF HERE!"

She slowly opened her eyes, and slowly turned her head about the room looking each person in the eye. To her left was Kyle and Brooke. Sitting at her feet was Bobby, and then Josh.

"I've asked for you all to be here today for a very important reason. Bobby, bring that box closer to me," Sarah said pointing to the box that Brooke had brought in. Bobby picked the bag up and leaned forward to hand it to Sarah. Josh grabbed it from Bobby as he knew that Sarah would be too weak to handle it herself.

"For many, many years I've been keeping a horrible secret. It's a secret that I am ashamed of, and one that I know will get me into trouble once I speak it." With that, Sarah opened the box and pulled out an old photo album, and opened it up. On the first page was a photo of Sarah and her brother, Raymond, taken when they were both younger. The condition of the picture told of its true age. The color was fading, there were some slight tears, and two of the corners had been bent. "This," she said pointing to her brother, "is my Raymond. He was my older brother, and only other sibling.

"Raymond and I didn't act the way most brothers and sisters do. We hardly ever fought, and with us living six miles from town, we were really the only friends that each other had."

Sarah turned the page to a picture which had four people posed in it. "Once Raymond finally got old enough, he got an apartment. Later Raymond and I shared it. It was great. We went out with friends, and once Web's opened, we were there every night. Did you know, I was the first waitress that your grandpa every hired?" Sarah asked Bobby.

"No, Grandma Sarah, I didn't." Bobby said looking surprised.

"I tell you, you get a group of men drunk and get a female in there with good looks waiting on tables, the money will just start to pour in. I was one good looking woman back then, and not too bad looking today," Sarah chuckled.

Everyone in the room let out a quiet laugh, but came quickly back to a silence.

"Who are those people in the picture with you Sarah?" Josh asked pointing to the photograph.

"On the far left is Andy Woelo, then me, and Raymond." Sarah stopped just staring at the last person, almost like she was trying to remember who it was.

"Mom, who's the woman on the far right?" Kyle asked.

"A horrible woman. I told Raymond that she was nothing but trouble. She was a tramp, and was sleeping with just about every man in town. Both married and single."

"Is that's Raymond's wife?" Bobby asked.

"Yes," Sarah answered coldly.

"What's her name?" Josh inquired.

"Her name *was* Beth," Sarah said as a smile cracked from her expressionless face. It made Sarah happy referring to her in the past tense, as if Beth was no more.

Everybody just turned their head to look at each other. They were beginning to think that they were getting more than what they had bargained for.

Sarah continued to flip through the book looking at all the pictures. She kept on saying something, but her words were muffled, and no one could understand what she was saying. After getting half way through the photo album, she shut it, and laid it off to the side. Sarah then reached back into the bag, and pulled out the old shoe box she had been looking at just a day earlier.

"Inside this box is why I have asked for you all to come. After keeping this secret from everyone, I feel that the time has come for the truth to come out." With that, Sarah pulled the top off, then by lifting the edge of the shoe box from underneath, she tipped it over. A pile of old newspaper clippings came pouring from the box.

"I want you all to look at these," Sarah said spreading the papers about her hospital bed. Everybody picked up a newspaper clipping.

"These are all on your brother's trial," Brooke said as she skimmed one of the articles.

"I know," Sarah replied.

"I don't understand Sarah, what does your brother's trial have to do with your big secret?" Josh asked.

"The only thing these articles report is the way everybody thinks the murder happened." Sarah said. All eyes and ears were focused on her. "Okay Bobby, you ready for the story of a lifetime?" Sarah asked, her eyes focused on his. Slowly Bobby shook his head yes.

"My dad had an affair on my mom early on in their marriage, and divorced soon after that. My mother should have never been a mom, so one day she got sick of Raymond and me, and ended it all. Dad had moved to Candletop after the divorce, and then back to Sumertown when mom died.

"He was a good father, when he wasn't drunk that is. Whenever he was drunk, he just never came home. He was usually spending the night at one of his lady friend's house. So, that meant for much of my life, Raymond was left to raise me, and did a good job of it.

"After Raymond and I got our own place together, Raymond had decided to work as a traveling salesman. This usually meant that he would go out of town to sell some of his products. He had a gift, he was able to make somebody buy something, even if they didn't need it. He was so powerful with his words, and that's why he was so successful."

"Grandma Sarah, how did your mom die?" Bobby asked.

Kyle was beginning to get a little upset as he felt Bobby was beginning to get a bit to nosy. "I really don't see that my mother's childhood has anything to do with why she has asked us here," Kyle commented in an upset manner.

"Kyle, it's okay. It is probably best if I just start from the beginning, that way, things might make more sense later on." Sarah answered. She was beginning to realize how complex this was, and how hard it was going to be to explain everything.

3
THE EARLY YEARS

Sarah laid on her bed, thinking. All at once a flood of memories came to her, all from her childhood. In the beginning, Sarah and Raymond had come from a good home. Their father worked in the factory, and their mom was a homemaker, and home schooled her children.

There was a seven year age difference between Raymond and Sarah. Everything seemed to be okay, until Sarah and Raymond's father was caught with another woman. Their parents divorced and their dad moved to Candletop, a small town of about seven thousand people, with his new love. Raymond was twelve, and Sarah was only five.

Life became rough for the three of them, Sarah recalled. She told all of her visitors how their mom went into a state of depression. The house went to hell, and she was no longer teaching her kids. Raymond was the strong one of the family, even at such a young age. So, he took it upon himself to teach Sarah everything that he already knew.

On a hot July afternoon, Raymond had made lunch for him and his sister and had decided to take it outside to eat.

Their back yard was filled with large oak trees which provided a great relief from the summer heat. As the two of them began to eat their bologna sandwiches, what sounded like a gunshot came from the inside of their home.

"What's that loud noise?" a young and frightened Sarah asked her brother.

"I don't know, it sounded like it was one of Daddy's old guns," Raymond answered looking towards the house. Sarah perked up thinking that their dad had come home, as it had been a year since he left.

When their dad was still living with them, life almost seemed perfect. With him working at the factory he brought home good money. With the left over money that they would have, their dad would always buy guns; he was fascinated with them. After the divorce he didn't bother taking anything with him. He just left town with the clothes on his back.

All of his guns were proudly displayed in a glass gun case in the living room. Raymond had begun to fear the worst had happened as he knew how unhappy his mother was.

"You stay right here, I'm going to go inside real quick," Raymond told Sarah as he pointed his finger at her. Sarah shook her head yes, and Raymond began to get up slowly from where the two of them had been sitting. Raymond began to walk towards the house as the sun cast shadows of the leaves on his face.

Raymond walked up the five steps that led to their back porch. With each step, the old wood would creak beneath him. Once to the top he turned around to make sure that Sarah was still where he had left her. When Sarah saw him turn around, she raised her little right arm high into the air and began to wave as hard as she could at her brother. Raymond gave a slight wave back to her and cracked a fake smile at her. He was afraid what he would find when he walked into the house.

Raymond opened up the screen door and stepped into their kitchen. He let the screen door slam behind him as he walked across the kitchen floor. It was really hot in their house, and the sweat began to bead up on Raymond's forehead.

"Mommy," Raymond called out from the kitchen. Only silence. Raymond then proceeded to walk into the living room and saw that his father's gun case had been opened with a gun missing.

Raymond walked from the living room to the hallway. The first room was the bathroom on the left-hand side. The next room down was his and Sarah's room also on the left. All the way down at the end of the hall and on the right side was his mom's room, the door open.

Raymond's heart was now racing, as he slowly peeked his head into the room. On the other side of the bed, on the floor, he just saw two legs. Tears began to fill his eyes as he entered the room. He noticed the wall had been painted red with blood right above his mom's body. As he stood at her legs, his worst thoughts had come true. There on the floor was his dead mother, one of his dad's rifles, and a broom, normally kept in the kitchen.

Raymond immediately ran out of the house and grabbed his little sister. "Come on, we have to go to town," Raymond said to his sister, pulling her by the arm.

"Waymond, it's hot, I don't wanna go," Sarah said as she was being pulled. Raymond didn't say anything, so in the scorching heat, he and Sarah began their six-mile walk into town.

Raymond didn't tell Sarah why they we were going into town, the only thing that she was worried about was how hot it was that day.

Sarah went on to say how they didn't get into town until almost ten o'clock that evening. Raymond had ended up carrying his little sister for half the way. The two of them stopped in at the Mom and Pop Shop and Raymond had told the owners what had happened. Raymond really didn't know anybody in town, he had only been to Sumertown a few times. His mom was the one who was always in town. She had started working at a small clothing store where she would fix tears and what not.

After Raymond had told the elderly store owners what had happened to his mom, the woman took the two of them to the back of the store and gave each of them a peanut butter and jelly sandwich, and a Coke. Sarah was really excited because she had never had soda before.

The elderly woman stayed with the kids as her husband went down the street to the sheriff's home. Sheriff Joseph Casper was asleep in his house when he was awakened by a knocking on the door. Casper was not one for turning heads. He was in his fifties, going bald, and a beer belly. He answered the door in only his pants.

"What's you need grandps?" Casper asked the elderly gentleman. Casper was a smart ass, and not very many people in town liked him.

"Sheriff, do you know the Turner's, live about, oh say five or six miles outside of town?" The elderly man asked.

"Yeah sure, the little lady works over at Jenny's, that, ahh, clothing store."

"Yes sir, that's the one. Anyways, her kids are here in town, down at the shop with my wife in fact. The boy says that he walked into the house and found his mom dead."

"What? Oh shit, I don't need this crap now, I'm tired. Give me about ten minutes to get dressed, and I'll meet you down at your store."

With that, Casper shut the door, and the elderly man began to walk back to his store. Once back inside his store, he found his wife sitting on a chair holding Sarah who was now fast asleep. Kyle just sat at a table, not moving. The elderly man came up to the table and told him that the sheriff was on his way out.

After a fifteen minute wait, Sheriff Casper came into the store, and he and the elderly man left together to go and have a look at the Turner's house. They didn't return until 12:30 in the morning. By now, both Sarah and Raymond were asleep, and the elderly woman was busy getting her store all cleaned up. When the two of them walked thru the door, both of their faces were as white as a sheet.

Sheriff Casper had asked if they would mind keeping the kids until he was able to contact their father. Both were more than willing to help. So, the elderly couple took both of the kids home with them and tucked them into their bed.

"What happened?" asked the wife.

"That poor boy. For him to walk in and see his mother like that was just horrible. She killed herself. Looks as though she put the riffle right up under her chin, and used the end of the broom to press down the trigger," answered her husband. There was no more talk for the evening so the two laid in each other's arms on the couch and went to sleep.

The next morning, Casper called over to the Candletop police station to see if they could track down the kids' father. As it had turned out, their father was in jail, and was always ending up there. Harold Turner was constantly in jail for his drunken habits. The sheriff of Candletop released him over to the deputies of Sumertown who took him back to town.

Once back in Sumertown the deputies took him to the court house where he met with Sheriff Casper, and Judge John Lynch.

"Have a seat, son," Judge Lynch said to Harold. "Do you know why we've brought ya in?"

"No sir," a hung over Harold answered. He was extremely tired now, and his head was pounding.

"Well, I was awaken last night at 10:30, turns out your kids ended up in town. We went over to your place and found your ex dead in y'alls bedroom. She done blew her head right off, and it was your son that found her," Casper explained. "Now, these kids need their father, so I would suggest you straighten up your act and take these kids back to Candletop with you."

"Can't do that," Harold answered.

"And why's that son?" asked Lynch.

"I've got nothing there for me. No house, no job, no nothin'. I think that it's just time for me to move back here and pick up right where I left off."

"That don't sound half bad," replied Casper. "I know they could still use some help down at the factory, hell, you were one of the fastest people that they had out there."

"Son, I suggest you pick up your kids and go on home. Bobby Rae has already picked up the body, and she'll be buried first thing tomorrow morning. Go home, don't you let your kids near that bedroom until you've had a chance to clean it up ya hear? And first thing Monday morning, you go down to the factory and see about getting your old job back." Lynch demanded.

"Yes sir, uh, just one thing, where's my kids?"

"Down at the Brady's, you know, the ones that run that Mom and Pop Shop when you first come into town. You can find your kids with them," answered Lynch.

Harold got up, thanked them both and left. He couldn't believe what Laura had done. How could she kill herself, how could she have been so stupid? Then he stopped, this was all his fault. Everything had been fine until he started messing around. Harold began to feel sick to his stomach. A huge amount of guilt overcame him.

"DADDY!" an excited Sarah yelled as she ran into Harold's arms. "Oh Daddy, I missed you so much. Mommy is going to be so happy when she sees that you're home!" Sarah kept giving her dad kisses on the cheek.

"Ahh Sarah, it's good to be holding you again," Harold said as he hugged his little girl.

"Hey there Raymond, did you miss me?" Harold asked as he set Sarah down.

"Where've you been, we needed you?" Raymond asked his father. It was apparent that Raymond wasn't quite as happy to see his father as Sarah had been. Raymond was old enough to be upset, to understand what was going on, old enough to hold a grudge.

"I've been really busy boy, and don't you shoot your mouth off to me. I'm your father, and damn it, you better start showing some respect boy."

"Were my father," Raymond said as he walked past his dad. In a quick flash, Harold yanked Raymond around by the arm, and smacked him across the side of his face. Sarah threw her small hands up over her eyes and began to cry.

Raymond's eyes began to water up, but didn't want his father to see that he had hurt him. He wanted to show his father that he was a bigger man.

"Boy, so help me God, you ever speak to me like that again, you'll be joining your mama in hell. Now let's go, and you quit your crying." Harold scolded to Sarah as he led them both outside of the house. They got into his old pick up which the sheriff had driven over earlier that morning, and the three of them went home.

Harold tried his best to make up to his kids for everything that he had already done to them. Every morning he would have breakfast ready for them. He would then drive the kids into town with him as they went to school and he would go to work. Once school would let out, Raymond and Sarah would go down to the Mom and Pop Shop to wait for their dad to get off work. Once he did get off, he would pick his kids up, take them home, and make supper for them.

Sarah was starting to enjoy this. For awhile it took her mind off of her not having her mom around. But every once in awhile she would ask where her mom was, and the three of them would get into the truck and go down to the cemetery.

For the first couple of years, Sarah and Harold were becoming more and more closer, while Raymond and Harold grew further apart. This didn't bother Harold. "If he wants to be a stubborn ass, then let him!" Harold would always say.

As time went by, Harold's old habits began to come back to him. He first started off by having a few drinks, and then came the women. By the time Raymond graduated from high school he was nineteen, and had been helping out at the Mom and Pop Shop just about every weeknight and on Sundays. He had saved all his money in the bank and once he graduated, he moved into Sumertown and got a small one bedroom apartment. For graduation, Harold had given his son the old beat up truck. Raymond was thrilled with this, and thought that was the only good thing that ever came out of his dad moving back to town.

Sarah, on the other hand, wasn't doing as great. She was now twelve, the age at which Raymond was when Harold moved back. And for the first time in her life, she was able to see what she couldn't seven years ago.

There would be times that Harold would never come to pick Sarah up, so Raymond would usually take her home after he got off at the shop. As it turned out, Harold was usually spending most of his time, and money, down at a tavern. Sometimes he would bring a woman home with him, sometimes he went to the woman's house.

This worried Raymond. He didn't like the thought of Sarah being at home by herself living so far from town. Plus, he didn't trust his father. What if he came home one night totally pissed off, would he hit Sarah? What if it went further?

It had been five months since Raymond had graduated from high school, and he felt that there should be a change in the way things were done. So, one day on his lunch hour Raymond went down to the factory to have a talk with his father.

"Yeah, hi, I was wondering if I could speak with Harold Turner?" Raymond asked a young lady that sat behind a counter. She wasn't very professional as she sat behind a desk chewing gum and filing her nails.

"That would all depend," she said as she blew a bubble. "What's your business with him?"

"He's my father," he hated saying that. "I really need to talk to him, family business."

"Hold on," she said as she pushed herself away from the desk. She opened a door that appeared to lead to where the actual factory work was being done. A loud construction noise came from behind the door. As the door closed there was a total silence. The only thing that could be heard was the second hand ticking on the clock that was hanging from the wall.

While Kyle was waiting he wondered about the small factory office, reading some of the things that were hanging from the walls. A lot of the stuff talked about how the factory had been started, and what all the factory built. While he was reading over some of the papers, he heard the loud construction noise again. He turned around to see the same young lady walking through the door with Harold.

"There he is, that's the one that asked for you," she said to Harold as she pointed to Raymond.

"Why don't we take this outside," Raymond said to his dad as he walked out of the building. Harold followed behind him.

"Shit boy, I figured once you left home I'd never see you again," Harold said while wiping his hands with a rag.

"Look, I'm going to make this quick for you. You're never home anymore, and you always forget to pick Sarah up at the shop. I don't like the idea of Sarah staying at home by herself, and frankly I don't trust you." Raymond said staring his father squarely in the eyes.

"If you've got a point, hurry up and make it. I've got things to do," Harold replied.

"I want Sarah to move into town with me." For a moment there was only silence between the two of them. Raymond felt good about himself right about now. He was able to stand up to his father, speak his mind, and for once not get hit because of it.

"Fine, I don't care. You think it's easy raising a girl, then be my guest. Hell, she's turning out to be just like you anyways. Nothin' but a jackass!" Harold yelled to his son.

Before Harold had the chance to turn around and walk off, Raymond made a fist and as quickly and as hard as he could, swung his fist around and punched Harold in the jaw. Harold fell to the ground, his lip bleeding.

"A word of advice Harold, don't you ever say anything bad about my sister again." And with that, Raymond got back into his truck and went back to work.

Later on that afternoon, Sarah came into the shop as she usually did after school.

"All right, you ready to go home?" asked Raymond.

"Don't you think that I should give Dad a few minutes before we assume he isn't going to show up again," asked Sarah as she began to laugh.

"I actually went down to the factory and had a talk with him today," Raymond replied. Sarah couldn't believe it. She, like her father, had figured that once Raymond left the house, he would never speak to Harold again.

"And?"

"You're moving in with me," Raymond said as a big smile came across his face.

Sarah ran up to her brother and threw her arms around his neck as she started to cry. "Thank you so much. I hated it there. Every night I've been praying that you would come and rescue me, and you did," Sarah said as she continued to cry.

It was going to be perfect. Sarah would be right there in town, and wouldn't have to worry about a drunken father coming home, nor would she have to worry about spending her nights alone.

Raymond got off work and he and Sarah drove to their father's house to get all of Sarah's belongings. She really didn't have all that much. A dresser, night stand, bed, and clothes. They were able to fit everything in the bed of Raymond's pickup truck. As Raymond shut the tailgate, he looked to see Sarah standing in the front yard, staring at the front of the house.

"It wasn't always bad in there," Sarah said still looking at the house they were leaving behind. "I can remember all the fun that we would have, especially in the back yard."

Raymond just smiled as he listened to his sister reminisce about the past. As Sarah went on to talk about all the fun she had, Raymond also started to remember. He had a few good memories, back when it was the whole family. And he could also remember all the fun times that he and Sarah had shared. But the one memory he would never forget, the one that he would take with him to his grave, was the one of his mother. If he closed his eyes, he could still see her body laying there, drenched in blood, her head practically gone.

"Raymond, come on. Let's get out of here," Sarah said giving him a slight punch on the shoulder. Sarah quickly climbed into the passenger side of the truck as Raymond climbed in the other side. With one last look in his rear view mirror he started his truck and they both drove away.

Once they returned to Sumertown, Sarah could hardly contain her excitement. She had never had a chance to see Raymond's place because whenever her dad would forget to pick her up, Raymond would simply take her over there as soon as he got off work. His apartment was right off the main street, two blocks down from the court house.

"Well, there it is," Raymond said looking up at his apartment. It was an old building that held four small apartments in it. "Come inside and I'll show you around, then we'll come back and get all your stuff."

The two of them climbed out of the truck. They walked around to the back side of the building and climbed a flight of stairs. At the top of the stairs was Raymond's apartment with the number 2A painted on his door. Raymond put the key into the lock and turned to unlock the door. When Sarah walked in, her face said it all, this was defiantly not what she was expecting. The apartment was very, very small.

"Okay, well you're standing in the living room slash dining room, over to your right is my full working kitchen. Hold your excitement Sarah!" Sarah tried to crack a smile. "And straight ahead is my bedroom, and to the right is the bathroom. Ta-Da!" Raymond said as he spread his arms out. "So what do you think?"

Sarah definitely thought that it needed a good cleaning job, and a woman's touch. "It's nice Raymond, but where am I going to sleep?"

"Oh, you're going to sleep in my room, and I'm going to take the couch."

"Raymond that's not fair. It's your house, I'll take the couch."

"No you're not, besides, you're becoming a young lady. You'll need room for all that womany stuff," Raymond laughed and gave his sister a hug. "Come on, let's get your stuff."

* * * * * * * * *

"Raymond was the best," Sarah continued telling her listeners. "He was everything to me. He was my hero!"

"Mom, you never told us that your dad was like that," Kyle said to his mom.

"I didn't see the point in talking about a father that, for most of my life, I didn't have."

"So, how did the apartment work out?" asked Bobby.

"It was great. After a few nights of Raymond sleeping on the couch, he found out how uncomfortable it really was. So, he ended up moving back into his bedroom with me." Sarah began to laugh.

"What's so funny?" Brooke asked.

"To give me my privacy, Raymond had gotten a large rope from the hardware store and hung it on both walls so it stretched across the room. Then he got this white sheet and would hang it over the rope, this divided the room in half. His part of the room had the door, he was kind enough to let me have the closet. It sure was great living with him. He would always make sure that I was up and ready for school. I was close enough now to school that I could walk. Raymond usually drove me whenever it would rain, or in the winter."

"Did the two of you ever talk to your dad?" Brooke asked.

"Once in a blue moon he would show up at the school, and on his birthday I usually went down to the factory with a card and cake that I had made for him. But Raymond, never. If they ever saw each other they would act like total strangers to one another, which is all they were to each other."

"How long did you live with your brother?" Bobby asked.

"Until a few weeks before he got married."

4
STIRRING THE POT

"But I'm getting ahead of myself," Sarah continued. She let out a yawn as it was now almost noon. "Once I graduated from high school, I got a job helping out at the court house. I did the basic secretarial work. Once Web's opened in '47, I was there."

Sarah wasn't old enough to work at Web's when it had first opened, but with Sumertown being such a small town nobody ever said anything. Besides, Sarah could have very easily passed as a young lady in her mid twenties.

John Maxwell ran ages with Raymond, in fact, the two of them had graduated together. John was the only one of the twenty-three graduates that left Sumertown. He always said, "I'm gettin' the hell out of here, and I ain't ever lookin' back." John had been gone for a good six years when he did eventually come back, and when he did, he had money. He told everyone that he had worked for a large corporation and how he had helped them to more than double their profits in such a short amount of time. So when he ended up quitting, they gave him a lump sum check as a thank you gesture.

Of course most of the town didn't believe John's story. Rumors began to make the rounds and people were saying that he was involved in a bank robbery that had occurred in Alabama. John really didn't care what everybody thought. He just knew that with all this money that he now had, his dream of opening his own business would finally come true.

So, as soon as he made it back into town, he got started on what promised to be the best place for everyone to hang out. Very few people knew what it was going to be, and again the rumors began to fly like wild birds.

"I'll never forget how excited John was," Sarah recalled. "It was July 7, 1947 when Web's opened. Nobody in town could understand why John had picked such an odd name for his bar. He told everybody that it was because of all the spider webs he saw when he first opened the door to what would later become his own bar. You see, Web's used to be an old storage facility for the courthouse. Once the courthouse had added on all those extra offices in 1944, there was no use of this empty space. So it just sat there for two years until John made it back into town."

"When did you start working for Grandpa?" Bobby asked.

"Opening night," Sarah answered. "I could not believe how many people had shown up. We were busy serving drinks until 2 o'clock in the morning. That may not sound like much now, but in '47 it was unheard of. My job was to take orders from the people at the table and bring them back their drinks. I made so much money that first night in just tips, I thought that I had it made."

* * * * * * * * *

"Well Sarah, I think that it is safe to say that you have found your knack in life," John said to Sarah as he put his hand on her shoulder.

"Hey, as long as I keep making all this good money, I'll keep coming back," Sarah laughed.

"Hell it's late, you better be getting home, need a lift?" John asked.

"No, I'll be fine," Sarah answered as she walked across the floor towards the front door. "You know what's so funny, John?"

"What's that?"

"When you said that you were going to open your own business everybody thought that you were just full of hot air," John just smiled. "I think that it's about time somebody stood up to this town, you actually did what you said you were going to do."

"Yeah, everything except not coming back."

"But then how would you have been able to rub it in everybody's face? Well, I'll see you tomorrow," Sarah said as she left Web's, waving to John behind her as she walked outside.

John walked up to the door after she left and turned the latch to lock the deadbolt and started to get things cleaned up.

Sarah was now 19, and very happy with how her life was going. Ever since she left home she had been so much happier, and now with her working at Web's she could now have money to buy herself all the things that she had ever dreamed about.

The first year for Web's seemed to go by so fast. Web's was opened everyday of the week, except Sundays. John would open at six, and stayed open until that last person left. People would go there to drink, socialize and catch up on all the latest gossip. Sarah really enjoyed it because of all the money she was making. She spared no expense. She bought herself a brand new car, and only the finest clothes. Everybody down at Web's loved her.

John had decided that he needed more help due to the business they were getting. So he decided to hire Raymond to help him out at the bar. John also hired his girlfriend and future wife, Becky, to help out with the serving of the drinks.

The four of them made a great team. They always got along, never had a disagreement, and always had each other's back.

After Web's had been opened for four years, Raymond felt that it was time for him to leave. Raymond was always the type who wanted to be on the move. He was jealous of John after high school because he had the guts and courage to move away. So, Raymond became a traveling sales man. He would often make his trips to Atlanta, which was about an hour from Sumertown, or Candletop, three hours away. Granted it wasn't the most glamorous of jobs, but Raymond was happy since for some short amount of time he was able to get away from the town he dreaded so much.

There were no problems with leaving Sarah at home by herself now. She was now twenty-three, and more than capable of taking care of herself. Though that didn't stop Raymond from calling each night to make sure that his little sister had made it home okay.

Raymond spent a lot of time on the road. He would sell anything, and was good at it. He mostly enjoyed selling encyclopedias. He would always go up to the rich neighborhoods in the towns that he was in, and would usually sell several of the series. This was great for Raymond, because he would make good money from doing this.

Meanwhile, Sarah would be back in Sumertown working up a storm at Web's. It was during one of the times that Raymond was gone when Beth Roder had moved into town.

"Hey Sis, what's going on?" Raymond asked his sister. He was in Atlanta selling vacuum cleaners and had decided to call Sarah one morning to see how she was.

"You are never going to believe what happened," Sarah said excitedly.

"What?"

"John and Becky eloped last night!"

"WHAT?!"

"Yeah, they called me early this morning and told me. They're in Candletop right now, and are fixing to leave. I'm planning a huge reception at Web's tonight, you think you'll be home for it?" Sarah asked.

"Married?" a stunned Raymond asked.

"Yeah, so are you going to be home or what?"

"Well of course. I haven't really been doing too well on this trip anyway, so I'll be home in a few hours. What time is the reception?" Raymond asked.

"I'm planning on four, but swing by when you get back into town, that way you can help me," Sarah said.

"I'll be there. Married, I can't believe it," Raymond hung up the phone and jumped into the shower.

Sarah started making her way over to Web's. It was nine o'clock, and she knew that there was a lot that needed to get done. She had asked Mitchell, one of her old flings from high school, to call everyone up and invite them to the reception later on that day.

Sarah got to Web's and unlocked the door. She didn't bother locking it behind her as she knew that Mitchell would be there shortly helping her get things all set up.

Sarah made her way back to the back of the store and started to put some wine bottles in the refrigerator so that they would begin to cool. While she was doing that she heard the bell ring from up front. She knew that someone had opened the door because there was a bell located on the doorframe. As the door would open, it would hit the bell.

"I'm back here Mitchell," Sarah yelled. She thought that it was too soon for Mitchell to be done, but then thought that he might have come over to start bringing supplies. After about thirty seconds she began to realize that Mitchell hadn't come back yet. Sarah walked up to the front of the store and saw a very attractive young lady standing on the other side of the bar. She was roughly 5'2, 120 pounds, blue eyes, long blonde hair.

"Oh I'm sorry, we're closed right now," Sarah said to the young lady.

"I apologize. I just moved into town a few days ago, and thought that I would check things out. Everybody tells me this is the place to be," the young lady said.

"It sure is, especially tonight. Our owner just got married, and we're throwing a surprise party for them later this evening."

"Oh that sounds like a lot of fun," the young lady said as she pushed her blonde hair off of her shoulders.

"You know what? I think this would be a great way for you to meet the people of Sumertown. You should come tonight."

"I don't think so, I wouldn't want to be rude."

"That's crazy, you're coming. It'll be a lot of fun. My name is Sarah," Sarah said as she stuck out her hand.

"Beth, Beth Roder," Beth answered as she shook Sarah's hand. "Would you like some help?"

"Would I ever! It would be a huge help if you could arrange this bar so that you can fit several hundred people in it."

"No problem, I'll be happy to help."

"Great, well, if you need anything, I'll be in the back." Sarah said. She turned around and began to walk back to the back of the store. She was finishing up with the rest of the wine when she heard the bell ring again. This time she knew it had to be Mitchell.

"I'm sorry sir, but we're closed," Beth said to Mitchell as he walked into the bar.

Mitchell was a very tall, very handsome man. He and Sarah had a thing in high school, but it didn't last long. Mitchell dumped her because he was a womanizer. He didn't like the idea of being tied down to just one girl. Sarah respected him for being honest, and not cheating on her. So the two of them had stayed very good friends.

"Well hello, and who might you be?" Mitchell asked Beth. Sarah began to laugh because she knew that Mitchell was about to go into one of his routines for trying to pick up a girl.

"That all depends on who's asking," Beth answered as she began to blush a little. Sarah was thinking to herself how much of a flirt Beth was.

"Mitchell, now you?" Mitchell replied.

"Beth Roder, I just moved to town...by myself."

Sarah almost busted up laughing. She gained control of herself and began to walk back to the front of the store.

"Mitchell, it's about time. So, I see that you two have already met," Sarah said giving Mitchell the calm down and keep it in your pant's look.

"We sure have," answered Mitchell. Beth just giggled.

"Right, okay. Mitchell, did you get a hold of everybody?" Sarah asked.

"Yeah, I sure did. I also got all those wine glasses, where do you want them?"

"Just set them up on top of the bar. I'll have to take them out of the boxes and get them washed.

"Okay, be back in a jiffy."

"He is cute," Beth said to Sarah as she fanned her face with her hand.

"He sure is, but be careful, I don't want you to get burned."

"Not unless I burn him first," Beth caught herself and looked out of the corner of her eye at Sarah. She noticed that she sort of had this look on her face. "Just kidding of course," Beth said.

"Of course," Sarah answered. She couldn't tell if Beth was being funny or serious. Sarah just pushed it off and thought there was still so much to do before the party than to worry about Beth's comments.

After Mitchell had carried in all the boxes, he began to help Beth with the table and chairs. Sarah was in the back again, this time washing glasses. Every once and awhile she would hear the two of them start to giggle. This didn't set right with her. Was it because she felt someone was moving into her territory? No, they weren't together anymore. Maybe she was just jealous because she didn't have anybody right now, maybe she still had feelings towards Mitchell. Sarah just took in a deep breath and finished up with the glasses.

At around noon, Raymond arrived back in town. He went to his apartment real quick to drop off all of his stuff and change clothes. After that, he headed down to Web's.

When he walked in he could barely recognize the place. All the tables had nice white table cloths on them. There was a huge congratulations sign that hung above the bar. Raymond knew that Sarah had made the sign, he could tell by the writing. There were even balloons all over the place. "John is going to think somebody has taken over Web's," Raymond thought to himself.

"Hello? Is anybody home?" Raymond asked out loud.

"There you are, I was starting to worry about you." Sarah replied as she came from the back. She went up to her brother and gave him a great big hug. "I've missed you so much, what took so long?"

"Nothing really. I ran home and changed that's all." Raymond answered. "John is going to shit when he sees this place. Table cloths, balloons, he's going to think that someone's trying to class this place up."

Sarah laughed and hit her brother on the chest. "Come back here and help me dry wine glasses. We've only got a few more hours until they get back into town. Did you eat lunch yet?"

"No."

"Good, I'm having Mitchell and Beth bring us over some sandwiches."

"Beth?" Raymond questioned with a hint of hmmm in his voice.

"Beth Roder, she just moved into town. Don't get no ideas though, I think that she and Mitchell are already an item," Sarah warned.

"Yeah but you know Mitchell, somebody else will come along in a few days, and poor Beth will need someone to cling to."

"Knock it off," Sarah laughed as she threw her brother a cloth. "Now, start drying these glasses."

The two of them began to finish drying the wine glasses. Raymond told Sarah about how his weekend had gone. He hadn't sold very many vacuum cleaners. Raymond went on to say how hard it is to sell them, and then began to tell her about all of the odd people that he had encountered.

"Sarah, we're back," Mitchell yelled out. Mitchell and Beth were carrying a large picnic basket as they walked into Web's.

"Good, I'm starved," Raymond said walking from the back.

"Raymond, I was wondering when you were going to be getting back into town. How've you been?" Mitchell asked. Raymond and Mitchell didn't know each other too well. Then once Raymond had worked at Web's for a while he got to know Mitchell, and the two of them had been friends ever since.

"Not bad, business was slow this time, but other than that I'm doing good," Raymond replied. "And who is this attractive lady?"

"Oh yeah, Beth this is Raymond, Sarah's brother. Raymond, this is Beth Roder, she just moved here," Mitchell answered.

"It's very nice to meet you," Raymond said to Beth as he shook her hand.

"Same here," Beth replied.

Sarah had come from the back and noticed the look on Beth's face. Being a woman, she could definitely pick up on the facial expressions and body language.

"So, what did ya bring?" Sarah asked breaking the silence.

"Roast beef sandwiches, they're my favorite," Beth answered.

"Mine too," Raymond agreed, even though they weren't.

The four of them all took a seat up at the bar, and Beth handed out the sandwiches and some fruit to everyone. Raymond went behind the counter and got everyone a soda. The four of them sat and ate their lunch in silence.

"So, yeah, when did you say John and Becky should be back in town?" Raymond asked. Finally something that they could all talk about.

"Around four, I told Mitchell to tell everyone to be here no later than a quarter after three. They have no idea that I've planned this. They just said that they would be back to work tonight and they were going to tell everyone their good news." Sarah answered.

"Quarter after three, I thought you told me a quarter after four!" Mitchell said shocked.

"What? No. Mitch, I told you that they would be back at four, not four…"

"Calm down Sarah, I'm just pulling your leg."

Everyone began to laugh. Sarah didn't see the humor in it, and just pushed it off. She noticed that Beth had seemed to think that it was extremely funny, and that she had an annoying high pitched laugh.

For the next couple of hours the four of them just sat around talking. They tried to find out more about Beth, but she just kept saying that she had left her past behind her, and that she never wanted to go back to it again. Sarah was beginning to think that she had done something pretty bad, and was afraid of getting caught.

Everyone from town began to arrive around two thirty, the rest by three. There were so many gifts. Everybody in town knew John and Becky, and also knew that they were the friendliest people in town.

Once it got to be a quarter of four, Sarah began to put the people in their place.

"Now remember, they have no idea that anything is going on. So, once they walk through the door, everyone yell..." Sarah started to say.

"SURPRISE!" It was apparent that they all knew their lines.

"Very good. They should be here in a few minutes. Beth, hit the lights." Sarah said.

Beth, who was standing next to the door, pushed the light switch down. It was beginning to get dark. It looked as though there would be a downpour at any minute as the sky was dark with clouds.

Quietly everyone waited. Four o'clock came and went. Four fifteen came and went. Four thirty came and went. Finally at ten till five, Sarah saw John and Becky walking down the sidewalk.

"Okay everybody get ready," Sarah said.

They could all hear John putting his key into the lock and opening the door to his bar. John flipped the switch up, the lights came on and, "SURPRISE!" everybody yelled.

"Oh my gosh," Becky said putting her hands up to the side of her face.

"What the hell happened to my bar?" John asked as he laughed.

"Well, you had to know that we would get back at you for not telling us that ya'll were getting married," Sarah said as she came up and gave John and Becky both a hug. "Congratulations you two," Sarah began to get all emotional.

"All right, let's start this party. Raymond, you wanna work for me tonight, you know, for old time sakes?" John asked.

"Anything for the newlyweds!" Raymond answered.

"Great! Everybody up to the bar, first round of drinks are on the house!" John yelled out.

Everyone broke into an applause and John and Raymond went to work making up drinks. Sarah went up and started to talk to Becky. Becky went on to tell Sarah how just at the spur of the moment they had decided to do this. Becky showed Sarah her ring, which had a decent size rock on it. As Sarah and Becky continued to talk, Sarah kept looking out of the corner of her eye and was noticing that a large group of men and gathered around Beth. Mitchell was up at the bar, so he had no idea what all was going on. And it was obvious to Sarah that she was leading them all.

"Would you excuse me?" Sarah asked Becky.

"Oh yeah, sure. I've got a lot of rounds to make with everybody," Becky replied. They both chuckled.

Sarah began to walk up to the bar so that she could get something to drink. Once she got up there, she turned around and leaned back on the counter and folded her arms across her chest. She just stared at Beth. There was just something about her that was rubbing her the wrong way.

"What you want Sis?" Raymond asked his sister.

"Just give me a cola." Sarah answered still staring at Beth.

"What's got you all in a fit tonight?"

"It's Beth, she's just...she's not right. I don't trust her Raymond," Sarah answered as she turned around.

"Jealous?"

"No, of course not."

"Are you sure? Now that there is some other new chick in town are you worried that nobody is going to like you?" Raymond asked.

"That's crazy. I know that I have nothing to worry about. Besides everyone will see through her."

"Maybe she's just trying a little too hard to fit in. Give her time, you two are going to be best friends. Now here drink up, I spiced it up a little for you, a put a cherry in it, ohhh," Raymond said sarcastically.

"Funny," Sarah said as she grabbed her drink. She began to feel a little warm, so she had decided to step outside for some fresh air. As Sarah made her way across the bar, she noticed that Beth was nowhere to be seen. She had figured that she had gone to the bathroom or something. Once outside, Sarah took in a long deep breath and let it out slowly.

The evening Georgia air was cool, especially this time of year, late October. Sarah loved to just sit out on clear nights and gaze at the stars. She was leaning up along the side of the building when she had heard some giggling coming from around the side of the building. She thought to herself that somebody was having a little bit too much fun, and was going to be nosy and see who it was. So, Sarah walked over to the far left side of the building, and slowly peeked her head around the corner. What she saw nearly made her come unglued.

There was Beth, making out with some guy. Some guy that wasn't Mitch. Sarah was pissed. She knew that there was something about her. And the nerve, for Beth to be doing this on her first night of getting to know everybody. Sarah immediately went back inside Web's.

She saw Mitch still standing up at the bar having a good ole time. She quickly walked up to him and tapped him on his shoulder.

"We need to talk," Sarah said to Mitchell.

"Can't it wait? We're having a blast!" Mitchell said as he raised a glass of beer over his head.

"No, we need to talk right now." Mitchell could see that Sarah wasn't happy.

"Okay, let's go." Mitchell followed Sarah back behind the counter and back to the back of the store. "So, what's up?"

"Are you and Beth an item?"

"What? Oh come on Sarah, please. High school was so long ago, we're over."

"I'm not talking about us. I'm talking about you and Beth. So, are ya?"

"Not that it is any of your business, but maybe."

"Well do you know where that tramp is right now?"

"You need to calm down Sarah,"

"Answer the question," Sarah's voice began to get loud, and her face was extremely red. It didn't take much to set off her temper, this was one of those times.

"She's out on the floor."

"No she's not."

"Yes she is."

"Mitch I just went outside and saw her kissing some other guy."

"You're wrong," Mitch said. He was beginning to lose his patience with Sarah.

"Mitch, I'm telling you."

"Listen here Sarah. Just because some new girl comes into town doesn't mean that you need to be starting this crap. Just because some girl likes me doesn't mean that you need to step in. I'm old enough to take care of myself. And I don't need you, or anybody else watching Beth's every move. So a bit of advice, butt out. Just mind your own business, and keep the hell out of mine." With that, Mitchell quickly turned around and went back out into the bar.

Sarah was stunned. In all the time that she knew Mitchell, he had never spoken to her this way. They were best friends. But why wouldn't he believe her? Why would she make something like this up? She was only trying to protect him.

Mitchell got back up to the front of Web's and was looking for Beth. He found her standing by the door talking to Andy Woeloh.

"Come on, we're leaving," Mitchell said to Beth as he grabbed her by the arm.

"Okay. Bye Andy, it was nice to meet you," Beth said with a wink of the eye.

"Like wise," Andy said.

Andy Woeloh was the sort of bad boy in town. His family had moved to Sumertown his junior year in high school, and it was then that he met Raymond. The two of them became best friends, and for the rest of their schooling, you would always see the two of them together. After high school was when Andy started to get into trouble with the law. Breaking into places, speeding, and picking fights. But none of this mattered to Raymond. Raymond always said that there would be nothing that would come between the two of them, that they would be friends forever.

Andy slowly made his way up to the bar, slowly strutting his stuff, thinking that he was all that. "Raymond, get me a beer," Andy said pointing to Raymond.

"What's got you so happy?" Raymond asked as he poured Andy a glass of beer and handed it to him.

"You know that new girl, Beth? Well, she and I were out in the alley all over each other." Andy said.

Just as he was saying this, Sarah had walked up from the back. "You son of a bitch!" She said as the reached across the counter and poured his glass of beer all over him. Sarah and Andy never got along, in fact, they hated each other.

"Sarah, what has gotten into you?" Raymond asked as he yanked the beer glass from Sarah's hand.

"Because of you and that Beth, Mitch thinks I made the whole story up. Now he hates me." Sarah said just glaring at Andy.

"Well ya know what Sarah, that's what you get for not minding your own business," Andy said as he got up from the bar. He quickly paced to the front door, and hit it hard with the palm of his hand to open it.

"Can you believe…"

"Don't Sarah. I don't want to know," Raymond was quick to interrupt her.

"Raymond you don't understa…"

"I may not understand, but I don't want to understand. Life is so much simpler when you look out for yourself."

Sarah just grunted and walked around the bar. She was so fed up with the people in this town. So, she decided to go on home. She walked outside of Web's and just stood there.

She hadn't realized that the weather had gotten so bad. A storm was on its way, and lightning was flashing all around her. She began to sprint down the street, hoping to make it home before it began to pour, but she didn't.

It was raining hard now, but she luckily only had a few blocks to go. Once she turned the corner she could see her apartment complex in front of her. She quickly ran up the stairs, skipping every other step. She put her key in the door, opened it, and turned the lights on. Finally, she could get out of these wet clothes. She shut the door behind her and began to walk towards her room when she heard a loud clap of thunder. Then only darkness.

"Damn storm," Sarah said out loud. It always seemed that with every storm, the electricity would go out. Sarah went into the bathroom, took off all her clothes and dried herself with a towel. She hung her wet clothes over the shower curtain and made her way back to her room. Once she got to her room she put on some pajamas, crawled into bed, and was trying to go to sleep. She just couldn't get her mind off of what had happened down at Web's. Maybe it wasn't Beth that she saw. Sarah knew that you could trust Andy just about as much as you could trust a kid in a candy store, but she felt certain that she had seen Beth outside. Sarah figured that the best thing for her to do was to apologize to Mitchell for what she had done, and hopefully, he would forgive her. With the storm still raging outside, Sarah went to sleep.

The next morning Sarah got up early, threw some clothes on, and headed out the door. It was Sunday, and everything in town was quiet. There was still a light drizzle and the wind made the air a bit nippy.

Sarah walked up to and across Main Street. Mitchell lived on Hallow Road, which was where Sarah was headed. She had been practicing all morning what she would say to Mitchell when she saw him. She was feeling better about herself, that is until she got to his house.

Mitchell lived in a small house. The outside of the house was peeling with old white paint. It was obvious how old the house was. But Mitchell was able to get a really good deal for it. Now if only he would fix the place up.

Sarah stood at his front door unable to knock. What was she doing there? She had no reason at all to be apologizing to him, in fact, it should be the other way around. So, Sarah began to slowly walk away from Mitchell's house when she heard something. It was the sound of someone unlocking a door.

"What are you doing here?" It was Mitchell. He was dressed in cut off sweat pants, and a white T-shirt. It looked like he had a little hangover.

"I came here to talk to you," Sarah replied.

"To talk to, or rub it in?"

Sarah was confused, what would she be rubbing in? "What are you talking about, Mitch?"

"Come inside before you catch a cold," Mitchell said to Sarah as he stepped back into his house. Sarah followed behind him and closed the door. She then sat down on a couch that rested on the wall that the front door was on.

"I got her here last night. We were just messing around and it was driving me crazy what you said to me last night," Mitchell started.

"I know, that's why I'm here. I just wanted to say…"

"Sarah wait. Just let me finish, okay?" Sarah nodded her head yes. "So, it was driving me crazy what you said last night and all. So I asked her if she had been outside with some other guy. She said yes, but they were just talking, nothing happened."

"Mitch that's cra…"

"Sarah, let me finish. She said nothing had happened, and I asked her who it was that she had gone outside with. That's when she told me she was outside with Woelo. I looked at her and said that she was lying. She said no, he told me that his name was Andy Woelo. I said no, you're lying about just talking. I went onto tell her that everybody knows that Woe doesn't just go outside to talk. If he sees a girl, then he wants the girl. She started to cry and boo the fuck hoo to me, and I told her that I didn't want to hear it. I told her that I never wanted to talk to or see her again. So she gathered up her shit, called me everything but a child of God and left."

Mitchell and Sarah just sat there for a moment looking at each other. Sarah was having mixed feelings on the inside right now. On one hand she was so happy. All along she had been right about this. And now, Mitchell looked like an ass because he wouldn't listen to his best friend. On the other hand she felt so sorry for him. He was such a great guy, and would never do anything to hurt anyone.

"So Sarah, for what it's worth, I'm sorry. I'm sorry I went off on you last night. I'm sorry I didn't believe you. I should have known better than that, and again I'm sorry."

"Mitch, it's okay, don't worry about it. Don't let somebody like her cause you such grief. For God sakes, you all had barely met."

"You are too nice, you know that?"

"Yeah I do," Sarah agreed.

"You want to go and grab something for breakfast?" Mitch asked.

"Why not," Sarah answered. So Mitchell put on some decent clothes, and the two of them went to the café for breakfast.

5
RUMOR HAS IT

A smile came across Sarah's face as what appeared to her guests was her remembering all the good times that she and Mitchell had shared together.

"Beth didn't stay around much after that day." Sarah began. "I think that after about three months she had completely left Sumertown. Nobody knew where she had gone to, and frankly nobody really cared. Everyone had figured that she had just picked up her stuff and moved on to her next play toy in some other town. The sad thing was we were all wrong, and her coming back would prove to be one of the worst things that has ever happened and would forever change and haunt my every living day."

* * * * * * * * *

Business at Web's was slow. A brand new theater had just opened up and everyone in town was taking advantage of both the picture and the air conditioning. It was now June 18, 1951 and the heat and humidity of the Georgia summer was just too much to handle.

Sarah and John were sitting up at the bar having a few drinks and talking about every subject possible.

"I say we just close," John said. "It's 8:30 and we have only had a few customers. Becky is at home and wants to go see that new picture they are showing in town so I say we just get out of here."

"Twist my arm," Sarah said as she spun around on the barstool and headed to the door. Right as she got there the door opened and in walked Andy. "Andy, we're closing up so you just need to come on back tomorrow." Sarah said as she patted him on the back.

The past year had not been very good for Andy. Both his mom and dad had been killed in an auto accident and ever since Andy was just not himself. Sarah had began to feel really bad for him. Although she did not have much of a memory of her mother, she knew how hard it was when her father wasn't always around. And ever since Andy had changed, Sarah had began to have feelings for him. It shocked her that she could ever feel this way towards Andy, especially after all the crap that he had caused. But she still had this feeling inside of her, one that she couldn't explain. Every once in awhile the two of them would go down and get something to eat at the diner, but that was about all.

"What do you say I take you to a movie and dinner?" Andy asked.

"Oh I suppose I'll go with you," Sarah said as she ran her finger under Andy's chin. "John I'll see you tomorrow," Sarah yelled back over her shoulder. John waved at her as he was finishing up getting everything put away. He didn't like the idea of Sarah going out with Andy. John knew that eventually Andy would stop mourning the loss of his parents and would eventually go right back to his old ways he was most famous for. John had told Sarah how he felt but Sarah was quick to back up Andy and she just knew that if he was with the right girl, her, then he would change his ways.

And it all seemed to be working just the way she wanted it. Raymond was gone a lot more now than usual. In fact, he was no longer living in his apartment. He had moved his stuff in with Mitch and would just stay with him whenever he was back in town. His traveling sales were really going along quite well and Raymond was making a lot of money. So for about a week and a half out of every month Raymond would be back in town. The rest of his time was spent out on the road. He found himself traveling outside of Georgia and seeing what America was first hand.

Since Raymond was gone all the time now, Sarah was feeling a little lonely. Most of her time was either spent at Web's, with Mitch, or with Andy. But here recently a lot of her time was being spent with Andy.

There was just something about him that she must have missed earlier. She was now madly in love, and by the time Christmas rolled around they were an item.

Word went around town about the two of them. Most people couldn't believe that Sarah Turner would ever go out with Andy Woelo. But as she would try to explain time and time again, Andy was a great guy and that he had changed. But that didn't seem to matter to Raymond and Mitch. Both of them were upset because they knew how Andy was, and the last thing that they wanted to see was for Sarah to get hurt by him. But she was a woman now, and could not be told what she could and could not do. So, if this was a mistake for her, then she was going to have to find it out the hard way.

The spring of 1952 was full of many surprises. The first was from John and Becky. The two of them were expecting, twins! Becky's due date was set for December 16, and Sarah immediately started thinking of all sort of names for the babies and how much fun they would be to have around.

The second surprise came on April 27 when Andy had Sarah over to his house for a romantic candle lit dinner. When Sarah came into his house all of the lights were turned off and on the table were two long candles that were lit. Sarah went over to the table and sat at one end of it.

"It sure does smell good in here," Sarah remarked.

"Hey, I didn't hear you come in. I'll have supper out in just a second," Andy replied from the kitchen. Moments later he came through the kitchen holding two plates of spaghetti, Sarah's favorite dish. He went back into the kitchen and brought back some sliced bread. "Now we eat," Andy said as he sat down across the table from Sarah.

"Everything is just perfect Andy, thank you so much." Sarah said as she took a sip of her water.

"Will you marry me?" Andy asked looking at Sarah in the eyes.

Sarah, shocked by this comment, began to choke and cough on the water she had just drank, "What?"

"Will you marry me? I have been in love with you for a few years. I knew that you didn't care much for me awhile ago, but I think that we both know that has changed. It's because of you that I have become a better person. So...will ya?"

"Yes!" Sarah answered. Andy went over to Sarah as she rose from her seat and gave her a big hug and a passionate kiss. "This is one of the best days of my life," Sarah said as she and Andy continued to hug.

* * * * * * * * *

"Mom, you never told me that you were engaged to somebody other than Dad," Kyle said looking at his mom in shock.

"Kyle, there are a lot of things that you don't know. The reason I never told you about Andy was because no one knew that we were engaged. I had told him that for the time being I didn't want anyone to know about it. After all everyone was against our relationship. We had agreed upon not letting anyone find out until after we got married. Our plan was to be married by the justice of peace in a small and simple ceremony in the summer of '53. It was going to be something that would never happen."

There was a tap on the door and one of the nurses came into the room carrying a tray, "Lunch is ready Mrs. McAlister."

"Tell you what Sarah, why don't we let you eat some lunch and we'll all go out and grab something to eat and be back in say an hour, okay?" Brooke said as she got up from her seat. It was obvious that she was ready to start talking to everyone and find out their personal input on what all they had heard up to that point.

"Oh I'm sure that'll be fine. Y'all go on now. Get some fresh air and we'll finish this in an hour," Sarah said as she lifted the lid off of her lunch and crunched up her nose. "Kyle, honey, would you bring me back some decent lunch?"

"You got it, Mom," and with that everyone got up and left the room. They walked down the hallway in silence to the elevator. Bobby pushed the down arrow and there was a ding with the opening of the elevator door. One by one they all got into the elevator and Josh, being the last one on, pushed the "G" button and the doors closed.

"Folks, whatever Sarah has to tell us has got to be something big," Josh said.

"There is something that I noticed while looking through all of those newspaper clippings," Bobby said. "The trial lasted only a day. Now I know that things weren't as hectic and as precise as they are today, but in a murder case, that just isn't right. And there was no jury."

"What was there to look at? You have a gun and Raymond in there with a body. That's pretty much an open and shut case," Kyle replied, thinking back to what he had remembered reading in one of the articles. Sarah had never discussed anything about the murder with Kyle. Sarah thought that was something that nobody needed to know about.

"What about an appeal? He was put to death the next day, just two days after the murder had been committed. It just doesn't add up. It's too quick, almost as if the judge was trying to get rid of him before something happened, or before something would be figured out," said Josh.

Once on the ground floor of the hospital, the four of them exited the elevator and proceeded to the front sliding doors of the hospital. They had all agreed to go to a little bagel shop that was located right next to the hospital. They all went in and placed their orders, and sat quietly down to lunch.

This is not what Brooke had in mind. She was hoping that they would discuss everything that Sarah had just told them. But like everyone else she found that she was at a loss for words.

Meanwhile back in the hospital Sarah just lay in her bed staring up at the ceiling. The lunch that was brought in for her was slowly getting cold. She couldn't eat anything, her stomach felt like it was tied in knots. Just thinking about what all had happened began not only to worry her, but also made her sick.

Dr. Stewards had walked into the ICU unit and approached the nurse's station where an elderly nurse sat working on her computer.

"How's Ms. McAlister?" he asked.

"Her vital signs haven't been doing too well. I've noticed that her heart rate has been on the increase over the past couple of hours. When I took her in some lunch I noticed that she looked a little pale and appeared to be breaking into a light sweat," the nurse answered.

Dr. Stewards turned to his right and looked down the hall to Sarah's room. He began to slowly walk towards her room and the closer he got to it, the more it sounded like he heard Sarah's voice. When he got to the door of her room he looked in and saw Sarah with her eyes closed saying something.

"Sarah?" Dr. Stewards asked as he lightly tapped on the door.

"GET OUT OF HERE!" Sarah yelled as she turned her head and opened her eyes wide at Dr. Steward. Just then alarms went off in both the room and at the nurses station as Dr. Stewards saw what appeared to be a lifeless body before him.

"Doctor, her blood pressure is dropping!" The nurse yelled as she began to run from the nurse's station.

After being gone for forty-five minutes Kyle, Brooke, Bobby, and Josh all got back onto the elevator and went back up to the ICU. As soon as they got to the floor, Kyle felt a strange feeling come over him as if something just wasn't right. As he walked down the hallway he began to quickly pick up his pace, almost to the point he was running. The others quickly followed behind him.

As soon as he reached the ICU and pushed open the doors he saw what he had felt.

"You need to get in there, she's taken a turn for the worst," said one of the nurses.

Kyle immediately ran down the hall to his mom's room followed by Brooke. Once they got into the room they saw Dr. Stewards putting some medication into her IV.

"She's been asking for all of you," he said.

"When did this happen?" Kyle asked.

"About five minutes after you all left. She went into cardiac arrest. Kyle, I'm sorry but this one was bad. Her heart is very weak."

Kyle went over to his mom's side and held her right hand. He saw his mother in the most painful way. Her silvery gray hair was matted down from what appeared to be a hard sweat, and she now had an oxygen tube feeding into her nose. Kyle was stunned. She was just fine no more than an hour ago and now she was dying right before his eyes. Brooke stood at the door unable to move, wanting to give Kyle a moment alone with his mother.

"Kyle?" A weak and tired Sarah managed to utter as she opened her eyes.

"Mom I'm here."

"Kyle where is everyone?"

"What?" Kyle couldn't believe what he was hearing. "Mom it's okay, just get some rest."

"No, it's not going to be long now. I can feel it." There was a short pause with no one saying a word. The only thing that could be heard was Sarah taking in very deep hard breaths of air, and the rhythm of the heart monitor. Then, "Please Kyle I have to finish. Go and get them before it's too late."

Kyle turned around and found Brooke already half way down the hall to get everyone. They ran back to the room and quickly took their places around the bed. Time was of the essence, and they had no time to waste.

"The following months are months that I have played over in my head time and time again. Just as Andy and I had discussed, we told no one about the wedding. That year, at the Fourth of July celebration, was when Beth came back into town."

* * * * * * * * *

"Well if it isn't the tramp herself," Becky said while eating a slice of watermelon at a picnic table. Sarah turned around to see who Becky was talking about and when she did she saw her brother walking arm and arm with Beth.

"What the hell is he doing with that bitch?" Sarah madly said under her breath. She got up from the picnic table and began to walk towards him.

"Where you going?" Becky asked.

"To have a little family talk." Sarah replied as she stormed over towards Raymond. She was so mad. He knew what had happened the night John and Becky had come back after their wedding. Why would he be doing this? The two of them were over at the barbecue grill getting some hot dogs to eat.

"Hey little sis, told you I'd be back for..." Raymond had started to say.

"I want to talk now," Sarah said as she turned around and began to walk away leaving Raymond no other choice but follow after her.

"It's good to see you again Sarah," Beth said in a fake cheerful voice. Sarah just kept on walking. In fact she was more pissed now because she had the nerve to even speak to her.

Sarah walked behind the dunking booth where Sheriff Casper was sitting. Needless to say he was not a very well liked man so there was a long line of people waiting their turn to dunk him. Raymond met Sarah behind there.

"I'm not even going to ask how it is that Beth ended up back here, but what I want to know is how the hell she ended up with you?"

"It's the funniest thing," Raymond said.

"I doubt that."

"I actually went door to door selling hand crème, and this one house that I came to was Beth's mother's house. But Beth was the one that answered. And ever since we've been together. She has been out with me on the road, keeping me company and now I've fallen for her."

"WHAT? Have you been sleeping with her?"

"That is none of your business. Keep your nose out where it don't belong."

"Just answer the damn question."

"Maybe I should be asking you the same thing about what is going on between you and Andy." Sarah slapped her brother in the face. She was ticked. For a moment they just stared at each other until Sarah pushed right by him and went towards Andy. That's when she saw him and Beth talking. This just wasn't her day.

"We're leaving," Sarah said as she grabbed Andy by the hand and pulled him away from her.

"Don't leave so soon guys, let's have some fun," Beth said.

Sarah immediately whipped around and got in Beth's face. "Listen here bitch, you keep away from Andy, he's with me now. And if I were you, I would just leave town and forget all of us and my brother. You hurt him and I swear to God I'll kill you." Sarah turned right back around and stormed away, Andy right behind her.

"You know what? You lose your temper way too quick," Andy said as they drove away from the fair.

"Don't start with me Andy, I'm not in the mood."

Andy drove Sarah home and figured that he himself should also just go home. He didn't want to get caught down at the fair talking to Beth, because he knew that it would spread around town like a wild fire. Sarah went on into her house and found Mitch sitting in her living room.

"What are you doing here?" She madly asked him.

"Raymond came back with Beth and I didn't want to be in the same house as them. You mind if I just bunk here for a week?"

"Is he stupid? Why, why, why? He knows what she is like, he knows all the crap that she started. Why would he do this?" Sarah asked as she plopped down beside Mitch.

"Maybe we're jumping to conclusions. I mean after all take Andy for example. He's done a complete 180 and now you're with him. Who knows, maybe Beth has done the same."

"I doubt that," Sarah said as she folded her arms over her chest. It didn't really matter what anyone was going to tell her. She was too mad to think of anything else or see any other version other than her own. "I'm going to bed," she said as she got up from the couch and walked back to her room. "Need anything?"

"Nah, I think that I'm going to go check out the fair. I hear there is a dunking booth with old Casper in it. After that speeding ticket he gave me last year I want my pay back." Sarah just chuckled as she went into her room and shut the door.

Early the next morning, Sarah got up and went into her living room where she expected to see Mitch sleeping on the couch. However she found that she was all alone in her house. She figured that Mitch had probably stayed and drank himself until he either passed out, or went home with someone else. She had some time to think things over and decided that maybe she had jumped to conclusions the night earlier and had decided to go over to Mitch's house and apologize to her brother. So she got dressed and started the walk to his home.

When she got there she noticed that Mitch's car was in the driveway, and that her brother's car was nowhere to be seen. So Sarah went up and knocked on the door. There was no answer. Mitch probably had a hangover and wasn't going to be getting out of bed anytime soon, but where was Raymond?

Sarah decided to go ahead and go down town to see if maybe he had gotten up as early as she did and grabbed some breakfast. She went into the local diner and found the place empty except for the elderly owners, Edith and Arnold Sheffield.

"Hey there Sarah, what can we get ya to eat?" asked Edith.

"Oh nothing for me Mrs. Sheffield. You haven't by any chance seen Raymond, have you?"

"Actually yes, he was in here late last night. Arnold wanted to stay open until after the fair was over in case anyone wanted to come in and get a little bite. But he and that one young lady, what's her name? The one that was here in town about a year ago and then left? Oh, anyways, they came in and got some coffee to go. He said that they were heading on to Atlanta that night, some sort business or something."

"Hmmm," Sarah replied. She knew that Raymond was still mad at her. He didn't even stay in town long enough so that they could talk things over. "Well thank you Mrs. Sheffield, you have a nice day. Tell Mr. Sheffield I said hi."

"I will Sarah. Bye now."

That explained a lot. Mitch must have run into Raymond at the fair and he told him that he wasn't going to bother staying in town because the two of them had gotten into a fight. Therefore he was going to go ahead and go on to his next sale.

Sarah went back to her house and just did some little chores to try to get her mind off of what had happened the night before, but she couldn't. She felt so bad for treating her brother the way that she had. He had always been there for her and she had just treated him like scum of the earth last night. She was hoping that he would call her sometime during the day, but the call never came. In fact it wouldn't be until December that she would even have the chance to speak to her brother again.

Andy and Sarah were walking around downtown doing some Christmas shopping when Sarah felt someone tap her on her shoulders. She turned around to see who it was and there stood Raymond.

"RAYMOND!" Sarah yelled as she threw her arms around his neck.

"Hey little sis, how are ya?"

"Oh God Raymond, I'm so sorry for what happened. I've missed you so much. How long..." Sarah looked up and saw Beth standing behind her brother. Sarah let go of her brother and just stared at Beth.

"We got married," Raymond said as he turned his head to Beth. Sarah just stood there. "I've decided that I'm going to let you have your say now, and then it will all be over with."

Andy came up behind Sarah and put his hands on her shoulders. "People can change," he whispered into her ear.

"I have only one thing to say," Sarah said as she walked past her brother and up to Beth. "Welcome to the family." Beth let out a long sigh and gave Sarah a hug.

"I know that we haven't always gotten along Sarah, but really, since I've been with your brother, I've changed. I want us to be friends." Beth said.

"Yeah, and we just got a house here in town," Raymond said.

"What!? When did this happen?" asked Andy.

"Last week. I'm going to be slowing down on my sales, you know try to start a family."

"I can't believe this," Sarah said as she hugged her brother again. "We should all spend Christmas together."

"Sounds good to me," Beth said. The four of them all decided to go over and look at Raymond's and Beth's new home.

Sarah was so happy. Her brother was back in town and she was able to forgive Beth for all of her wrongs. Christmas that year seemed like old times for Sarah. She was with her family and close friends. As Raymond, Beth, Sarah, and Andy all sat in Raymond's living room, there was a knock on the door.

"I wonder who that could be?" Raymond said as he got up from the couch to answer the door. When he opened it, he saw Mitch. "Mitchell," Raymond said. Their friendship had come to an end when Raymond starting going out with Beth and finally marrying her.

"Hey Mitch, Merry Christmas," Sarah said as she got up and gave him a hug. "You need to come by the house tomorrow and get your gift."

"Sounds good. Look I don't want to stay long, but I thought that I would let you know that Becky gave birth to a boy and girl."

"WHAT?" everyone yelled.

"Yeah, John just called me. He didn't know the number here so I told him that I would let you all know."

"What are their names?" asked Beth.

"Agnes and Tommy."

"Those are such cute names," Sarah said. "When can we go and see them?"

"They said that everyone can start coming to the house day after tomorrow. John is going to keep Web's closed for the next week."

"I can't wait to see those little ones," Beth said.

"Anyway, I'm going to get going," Mitch said as he turned around.

"I'll call you later Mitch," Sarah said. Mitch waved his arm as he walked away.

Two days later Sarah went to John and Becky's house to see their two new babies. As Sarah sat talking with Becky and holding Agnes it made her realize how badly she wanted a family. She knew that by the end of the summer she and Andy would be married, and then they would be able to have kids.

Sarah and Beth were getting along very well with each other. Usually before Sarah had to go into work at Web's, she and Beth would spend the day together talking, shopping, or doing just little odds and ends.

Raymond had stayed in town until the end of February when he started back up with his selling and was out on the road. He tried to only stay gone for just a few days at a time. He would usually leave town on Monday and try to be back home Friday night, stay the weekend, and be back out on the road Monday morning. Beth didn't seem to mind it too much. Usually her days were kept pretty busy with Sarah, but sometimes at night she would feel a little lonely.

Sarah had gone into "Curls" so she could to get her haircut. She always loved going there. The stories those old ladies would come up with would have you hanging on their every word. Also, they always had the best gossip in town and didn't care who was around to hear it. They had no problem gossiping about your own family as you sat in their chair.

The shop was run by two women in their late fifties, Doris and Bessie. Sarah patiently sat in a chair flipping through a magazine waiting her turn.

"Alright Sarah it's your turn Hun," Doris said. Sarah smiled and walked over to the chair by the sink so that she could get her hair washed. "How've things been going for you sweetie?"

"Just fine, I've been really busy."

"What about your brother, I ain't seen much of him?"

"He's back on the road selling whatever it is he is selling."

"You know what I heard?" Doris asked as she began to wash Sarah's hair.

"No, what?"

"I've heard that Beth and old judge Lynch have been sleeping together. Word has it that his wife has already left him and moved in with her sister back in Alabama."

Sarah was shocked. On the one hand she didn't believe it. She had been around Beth long enough to know that she had changed. But then on the other hand, she also knew what Beth had done in the past.

"Are you sure about that Doris?" Sarah asked.

"Hey, I simply tell it as I hear it. You better watch that little hussy. You know that nobody really cared much for her. In fact most women here would like to see her ran out of town." Doris wrapped Sarah's hair up in a towel and the two ladies walked over to one of the chairs and Sarah sat down.

She sat in that chair staring at her reflection in the mirror. Please let it all be a rumor. Please don't let any of this be true. Sarah couldn't get the thought out of her head. The more she thought about it, the angrier she got. She was nearly to the point of having the same feelings towards Beth as she had earlier.

Sarah sat quietly in the chair while Doris cut her hair and continued to gossip with all of her customers. By now the subject had changed from Beth to how much weight Dorothy Crumb had put on and just how much she had let herself go. Everyone but Sarah.

"No, it can't be true, it just can't. Okay Sarah, just think this thing through. She's changed, you've seen firsthand how much she has changed. Plus how could she forget how pissed you got with her. Surely she would use the brains God gave her, and she would have the common sense not to screw around while Raymond was out of town. No...no, no, no, no. I won't. I won't believe it." Sarah said to herself as she stared at her reflection.

Doris finished up with Sarah's haircut. "There we go, all done. You okay sweetie, you've barely said a word since you came in here?"

"I'm fine, just not feeling too good," Sarah answered.

"Well, there is that flu that started and I think Norma Jean's son was one of the first..."

"Doris, I'm sorry but I really do need to get going," Sarah interrupted.

"That's fine, just leave your money up there on the counter. Susie, you're next. I'll talk to you later Sarah," Doris said as patted Sarah on her shoulder.

Sarah left her money on the counter by the door and walked outside. For the middle of April things were beginning to really warm up. Across the town square, Sarah saw Beth walking down the court house steps with Judge Lynch. Sarah couldn't believe it.

That night at Web's, Sarah was busy getting drinks when Raymond came in. Sarah had noticed her brother but didn't take the time to acknowledge him. She was still pretty upset from everything she had seen and heard earlier that day.

"Well there he is, one of my best customers. How you doing?" John asked Raymond as he walked up to the bar.

"Not too bad. Figured I would grab a beer before I went on home to the ole ball and chain," Raymond laughed as he reached across the bar to shake John's hand. "Hey Sis, what's going on?"

"Nothing."

"Since when have you been the quiet type?"

"Look Raymond, I don't feel good and I'm busy. So just tell me what the hell you want to drink so I can get back to work." Sarah was fuming.

"Well, her monthly visitor seems to have stopped in," Raymond laughed. John couldn't help not laugh and joined in on the humor. Sarah was even more pissed now. She wanted so badly to tell her brother everything that she had heard, but it wasn't her place.

About that time Becky came up to the bar with a list of drinks.

"Becky, I need to go home. I feel like shit," Sarah said.

"I thought that something was up with you tonight. You go on now. John and I can handle this," Becky said as she gave Sarah a hug.

"Thanks I appreciate it." Sarah walked around the bar and walked out into the warm outside air. She just looked up gazing at all the stars.

"I didn't mean to upset you in there," Raymond said as he joined his sister outside.

"It's not you, I've just a lot on my mind that's all."

"Care to talk about it?"

"Not really."

"Well you know that if you ever need anything or just someone to talk to, Beth and I are always there for you." Just the sound of her name made Sarah's skin crawl.

"I know, and I appreciate it. Look I'm just going to go on home and get some sleep."

"You want me to walk you?"

"No that's okay, I'll be fine. Go on back in there before your beer gets warm."

"Alright then, if you're sure. I'll call you later," Raymond said to his sister as he walked back inside.

As Sarah walked home she began to think to herself how it was she would be able to find out the truth. It wasn't like she could really go and talk to anyone in town. Most people were probably tired of hearing her bitch and complain. Besides if she started to question people that would just start a new batch of rumors and people would start saying that she was jealous since her brother was spending more time at home with his wife than with his sister.

She finally decided that this was all crazy. It was probably just some stupid rumor that Doris or one of the other ladies had started. The time that Sarah spent walking home seemed to really help her nerves and to help her calm down.

* * * * * * * * *

"After that evening I decided to put all my hateful feelings and doubts towards Beth behind me," Sarah continued. "I swore to myself that unless I had proof I would no longer get involved or start jumping to conclusions. I didn't express my feelings to anyone about Beth. But I soon found out that as time went on, so did more rumors, a lot more rumors. It was the juiciest piece of gossip. Everyone was talking about just who Beth was sleeping with. I didn't want to believe what I thought were lies. I was talking to Beth practically every single day and she had seemed just fine to me. After all, I would have thought that a tramp like her would be very nervous talking to her husband's sister who has such a short temper."

6
REVENGE

"It's all so clear to me," Sarah said as she closed her eyes, as if to reach back to times that had gone by. "It was May 28, 1953, and around noon when Raymond had stopped by the house. He didn't look good. He looked very old and very tired. It was like he hadn't slept for days. His face was pale and expressionless and for a couple of minutes he just sat on my couch holding a cup of coffee, staring off into space. I couldn't stand the silence for very long so I just asked him..."

* * * * * * * * *

"Raymond, what's wrong?"

"Nothing really," Raymond said still holding his cup of coffee. "I just have a lot on my mind right now, that's all."

"It's got to be more than that. You said that you had something that you wanted to talk to me about." Sarah sat across from her brother waiting. Waiting for an explanation, waiting for him to tell her what was so important, waiting for him just to say anything.

"I think that there might be something going on with Beth." Sarah immediately sat up straight in her chair. She had been thinking that was the reason that Raymond had wanted to talk to her.

"Ok..." Sarah said wanting him to continue.

"We've been fighting. A lot. It's not the little stupid stuff, it's big, you know. We fight every time I go away on one of my sales trips. We fight whenever I get home. She always says that I'm not there for her, that she needs somebody to be with her all the time." Sarah didn't like the way this conversation was going. "So I asked her if she wanted a divorce or something. And she said yes."

For a moment there was nothing but silence between the two of them. Sarah was shocked. She had always thought that things were going just fine between Raymond and Beth, but she obviously was wrong.

"Is that what you want?" Sarah asked her brother.

"Whatever it takes. She's driving me crazy, Sarah. And there's one more thing," Sarah expected that there was more. "I think that she has been fooling around on me."

"WHAT?" Sarah yelled as she pushed herself up off the chair quickly.

"Now I don't know for sure, Sarah. I just, I don't know. We haven't, you know, in a few weeks. Yeah it's driving me insane but she seems alright with it. It almost makes me wonder if she isn't getting her pleasure from somebody else."

"Raymond what did I tell you? I knew it, I knew that she would try to pull something like this. What did I tell you?" Sarah was now pacing back and forth in her living room, fuming hot. She kept saying over and over, "I knew it," and throwing her arms up into the air.

"Sarah, I don't know for sure so just calm down. Look I'm going to Candletop and I'm probably going to be up there for about a week. I'm going to have to do a lot of thinking. I just need you to do me a favor."

"What is it?" Sarah asked still very upset.

"Find out for me. See if she is fucking some other guy. I really need this from you." Raymond asked in an almost poor, poor pity me voice.

"Alright I will. But if she is Raymond, so help me God, I'll kill her."

"No you won't. Just find out for me and I will handle the rest. Look I got to get going so I'll see you in about a week okay?" Raymond said as he set his coffee cup down and got up from the couch. He went over to his sister and gave her hug. "You know that you're the best."

"I know," Sarah replied. But her response was cold. There was only one thing on her mind and that was getting Beth.

As Raymond pulled away from Sarah's house, she had a million thoughts going through her mind. If this were all true, how could she have not realized it? She hadn't seen any physical proof as of yet, only heard rumors. It was going to take some serious work, but deep down Sarah knew that she would figure it out.

Her first step was to call Beth and see what she was going to be doing that day. Sarah figured that she would follow Beth around town, see what all she would do, she who all she talked to.

"Hello?"

"Hey Beth. How are ya?" Sarah asked as she spoke into the phone.

"Oh, hi Sarah. I'm doing good, you?"

"Not to bad. So what are your plans for today?"

"Not much really. Why did you want to do something?"

"Ah, no. Um, I'm actually pretty busy today. I was thinking of having a get together with a whole bunch of us when Raymond got back."

"Okay?" Beth sounded confused by Sarah's reply.

"So, I'm going to be busy trying to get the house clean and get some items together."

"Oh, you want me to come over and help?"

"Nah, I think that I can pretty much handle it. So, I guess that I'll talk to you later."

"Okay. Bye Sarah."

Sarah hung up the phone. Had she been too obvious? Sarah began to think some more. Her phone conversation proved to be useless. What now? She figured that she would go ahead and follow Beth.

Sarah left her house and went straight over to Beth and Raymond's home. She couldn't tell if Beth was home or not. So Sarah went around to the back of the house and looked through the kitchen window which was slightly opened. She saw that the T.V. was on but no sign of...wait. There she was walking around in the living room, and talking on the phone.

"Oh stop it, you know you want to." Sarah heard Beth say. "Look, nobody will find out, don't worry about it. I know, me too. Okay I'll come by say around five? Great, I'll see you then. Be ready for me." And with that Beth hung the phone back on the wall and walked down the hallway.

Who was she talking to? Maybe Sarah was getting somewhere. Who was Beth going to be meeting at 5 o'clock, and what was there not to be worried about? Sarah figured that she should go ahead and leave and had decided that she would come back closer to 5 and follow Beth to where ever and whomever she was going to meet.

Sarah began to walk home. There were a lot of things going through her mind right now. As she turned a corner she saw a lady leaving her front door, crying.

"Can I help you?" Sarah asked as she approached the lady. The lady turned around and it was then that Sarah knew who it was, Stacy Wellington.

Stacy Wellington was the lady that Sarah and Raymond's dad had been dating for the past two years. Sarah hadn't seen much of or heard from her dad since he had started dating Stacy. She was a very strong tough woman who always got what she wanted. She even got Harold to quit his drunken habits. Since he wasn't drinking any more Sarah never saw her dad down at Web's. The only time the two of them would ever have a chance to talk was if they ran into each other, and only if Stacy wasn't around.

Stacy didn't care much for Harold's kids, in fact she despised them. Stacy always thought that Sarah and Raymond didn't show their father enough respect. Harold was always good about backing his children up, even Raymond. Harold would always try to tell Stacy how he wasn't a very good father, and in turn he got what he deserved from his children. A daughter whom he would speak with every once in a while, and a son whom he hadn't spoken with in many years. Stacy's logic was that his children should forgive him for what he had done. Nobody in this world is perfect, and everyone deserved a second chance. Harold could do nothing to please Stacy in this matter, so Harold didn't get the chance to see Sarah all that much. So why was she at Sarah's house now? Sarah's feelings towards Stacy were quite mutual.

"What are you doing here?" Sarah asked as she folded her arms across her chest.

"Sarah," Stacy said as she sniffled, "it's your father."

Sarah just stood there. She was expecting Stacy to say something like "I can do nothing to please your father," or some bullshit like that. "What about my father?"

"Sarah he was put in the hospital this morning. He was in a horrible car accident. He's really bad Sarah, and he keeps saying that he isn't going to make it," Stacy said as she wiped her nose on a tissue she had pulled from her pocket. Sarah's own eyes began to tear up and she could feel a lump in her throat. "He's been asking for you and Raymond. He needs the two of you there."

"Then we need to go," Sarah said as she just looked all around in a panic. Almost as if she was lost and was trying to find her bearings.

"What about..."

"He's in Candletop. We need to go, now!"

Sarah got into the passenger side of Stacy's car while Stacy got behind the steering wheel. Quickly, Stacy raced towards the hospital as time was of the essence.

The hospital in Sumertown was a small one that had only ten rooms and an ER. Sarah ran thru the front doors of the hospital and immediately went up to the volunteer sitting behind the desk.

"I need to know which room Harold Turner is in."

"Let's see," the elderly lady said as she pulled on her reading glasses and began to slowly read off the names listed on a sheet of paper of all the people that were currently in the hospital. Sarah didn't have time for this.

"For Christ sake," Sarah said as she snatched the list out of the lady's hand.

"You can't look at that."

Sarah ran her fingers down the list and saw that her father's name was third to the bottom. "Room 6, Bed B." Sarah said as the she laid the sheet of paper back down on the desk and started running towards her father's room. By this time, Stacy had come into the hospital from parking her car.

"Miss, you cannot run in the..." the elderly lady had started to say, but Sarah was already too far down the hall to care.

As Sarah continued down the hall her eyes kept glancing at the room numbers. 1, 2, 3, 4, 5, and finally 6. She stopped right outside the door. Under the room number she saw her dad's name written on a chart. As she slowly entered his room she heard some of the machines that Harold was hooked up to beeping. His bed was the one by the window.

There was nobody else in the room with him and his head was turned as if he was looking outside.

"Dad?" A tearful Sarah called out as she went to his side and grabbed his left hand.

There was a slight moan and Harold turned his head to look at his daughter. Sarah nearly lost it, she could barely recognize the man in the bed. His face was completely bruised, swollen, and covered in cuts. "Hello, Sarah."

"Dad, you're going to be alright," Sarah said as she grasped his hand even tighter.

"Where's Raymond?"

"He's in Candletop all this week, Dad."

"Sarah I want you to listen to me," Harold said. At that same time Stacy walked into the room. "I'm not going to make it Sar..."

"Yes you are Dad, quit saying that."

"Sarah please just listen to me. They say that I have a punctured lung, and that I'm bleeding internally." Harold said looking painfully into his daughter's eyes. He thought to himself what a beautiful young lady he had for a daughter. "First, I know that I haven't been the greatest father to you or Raymond and I'm sorry for that. Secondly, I'm so proud of both you. You know I used to see you and Raymond all the time out doing something and I would think to myself, those are my kids." Sarah began to cry even harder now. "Third, I love both you and Raymond with all of my...all of my heart." Harold was now fighting for air as he began to slightly twist and turn in his hospital bed. You could hear him weazing as he gasped for each breath.

"Dad, I'm so sorry I wasn't always there for you. I love you so much." Sarah bent down and gave her father a hug while still holding onto his left hand. Harold slowly picked his right arm up and put it around Sarah's shoulders. Stacy stayed in the back of the room crying. She had an enormous feeling of guilt come over her. It was because of her that Harold had not had the chance to spend more time with his children.

Sarah continued to hug her father. Then she felt the grip in her father's hand loosen. At that time the beeping noise from his heart monitor went to a steady tone. Sarah looked up at the monitor and saw a constant line running across the screen.

"Dad?" Sarah said as she stood back up. "DAD!" Sarah began to shake her dad's shoulders. "No. Oh God no, no, please don't take him. Dad please come back to me, please!" By that time, two nurses had come into the room. One pulled Sarah off of Harold while the other began to perform CPR. After a couple of minutes they saw that there was nothing more they could do. The time of death was 2:03 p.m.

Sarah was sitting in the lobby of the hospital. For the first time in her life she was without a parent. Sure she didn't get to see much of her father, but at least he was there. But not now. While sitting there, many questions came to mind. Would she be responsible in planning his funeral? She hoped not. She wouldn't even know where to begin. What about Raymond? How was he going to take it? Sarah didn't want to be the one to tell him about their father. She could just hear it now, "What the hell took him so long?" If he was to say anything like that Sarah would find it very hard to forgive him. But he did have the right to know.

As Sarah continued to sit in the lobby she saw Stacy start to come over in her direction. Sarah noticed how hard she was crying. It was then that she realized how much her father meant to Stacy. As she got closer, Sarah stood up to talk to her and was shocked when Stacy gave her a hug.

"I'm so sorry," Stacy said. "You two meant the world to him. I'm so sorry that he is gone."

The two of them cried together and after awhile just sat and talked, trying to figure out where to go next. The two of them had decided on having a private funeral on May 31. Sarah had thought that would be good. This would give Raymond a chance to make it home if he wanted to go to the funeral.

After leaving the hospital, Stacy and Sarah went over to Harold's house and started going through some of his stuff and picking out which suit they thought he should be buried in. After spending a couple of hours together, Sarah and Stacy decided to go on home. Stacy had offered Sarah a ride, but Sarah declined yet thanked her for the gesture.

As Sarah walked home she felt lost and alone. She couldn't believe that her father was actually gone. While walking past the downtown square, Sarah heard the clock on top of the courthouse chime. She looked across the street at the courthouse to see what time the clock said, it was 7:00. Sarah continued to walk down the sidewalk when she heard giggling. That's when she saw Beth and Judge Lynch outside the courthouse together, again. She had completely forgotten about Beth and that "thing" she had to do at 5pm.

How could she? It was obvious that Beth was starting the divorce while Raymond was out of town. That was low. As Beth walked down the rest of the stairs from the courthouse and down the sidewalk, Judge Lynch began to make his way back inside the building. Sarah sprinted across the square and ran up the stairs and reached the top just as Judge Lynch opened the front doors.

"Judge Lynch," Sarah called out as she came up behind him. As he turned around he looked like he had just seen a ghost. Guilt was written all over his face. "Judge Lynch, what was Beth doing here?"

"I...I um, I can't discuss that with you Sarah, it's a...private matter." Lynch answered as he stumbled over his words.

"Is she trying to get a divorce from Raymond?"

"Sarah I said I can't discuss this matter with you." Lynch was much more stern this time.

Sarah's eyes began to tear up. All at once all of her emotions about this whole situation and that of losing her father seemed to be rushing out. "I'M SO SICK AND TIRED OF EVERYONE WALKING AROUND THIS FUCKING TOWN WITH THEIR SECRETS!" Sarah yelled. Her face was now dark red and she was having trouble catching her breath between her tears. Judge Lynch reached out to put his hand on her shoulder, but Sarah was quick to jerk away and ran down the stairs crying. Judge Lynch simply shook his head and went back inside the courthouse.

Sarah threw herself on her bed and could do nothing but cry. She felt like the world had turned its back on her and she was left all by herself to win a winless ,battle. It was now just past eight and she had realized that she hadn't called John to let him know that there was no way that she was going to be able to come in to work.

"Sarah is that you?" It was Becky who had answered the phone at Web's.

"Y...yes," Sarah whimpered.

"Oh, honey, I'm so sorry to hear about your father," Becky said. Pretty much everyone in town had probably already heard. "Is there anything that I can do for you?"

"Becky, there is no way I can come in, at least not until after the funeral."

"Don't worry about a thing. You just come back whenever you are ready, John and I can handle things until you get back. And remember, if you need anything you be sure to let one of us know."

"I will, thanks." Sarah hung up the phone. The only thing that she could do now was wait for Raymond to call.

Sarah went into the kitchen to make herself a cup of tea. There was a knock at the door. Sarah didn't even bother to go and see who it was. She didn't want to deal with anybody, at least not tonight. The person continued to knock three more times until they finally got the picture that no one was coming to answer the door.

Finally around ten that night, Sarah's phone rang.

"Hello?"

"Hey Sis, how's it goin'?" Sarah began crying again. She tried to tell her brother about their father but only mumbling came out because of her crying so hard. "Sarah, calm down. Take a deep breath and tell me slowly what happened."

Sarah took in a deep breath and wiped her eyes and nose. "Okay. Raymond," the tears started back up, "Dad was in a car accident this morning." Sarah paused expecting Raymond to say something, he was silent. "Raymond, Dad died this afternoon." Sarah began to cry hysterically.

"What?"

"He...he...he's gone Raymond. Oh God, he died in my arms Raymond. I can't believe it."

"Oh Sarah, I'm so sorry that you had to go through that." Raymond himself began to feel a little emotional. Mostly because of what his sister was going through. Raymond hated it when Sarah would cry, but deep down some of those tears were for his father. "When's the funeral?"

"It's the 31st. Are you going to be here?" Sarah asked hoping that he was going to say yes.

"I'll be there that morning, you can count on it."

The two of them continued to talk for a couple more hours. Raymond thought that he had better not bring up Beth under the circumstances, and after what Sarah had been through, she had completely forgotten about it. After the two got done talking, Sarah went and grabbed her blanket off of her bed and went back to the couch. She just lay there hugging the phone and still crying. After awhile, Sarah had cried herself to sleep.

Sarah nearly fell off of the couch. She looked across the room at the clock on the wall, it said 7:30. What had startled her? There was a knock at the door and that's when Sarah knew that was what had woke her up. She picked herself up off the ground and went over to the door and opened it. There stood Mitch.

"Oh Mitch," Sarah said as she wrapped her arms around his neck. "He's gone."

"I know Sarah," Mitch said cradling her back and forth. "I came over last night but you must have not been home."

"Oh sorry," Sarah said as she stepped back from him. "I heard someone at the door but I just didn't want to see anybody."

"Have you had a chance to talk to Raymond yet?"

"Yeah he called last night. He's going to come home for the funeral. You know I haven't heard from Andy yet, you haven't seen him have you?"

"No I haven't. He's probably just giving you your space. I'm sure he'll either call or stop by today."

"You're probably right. I need to get dressed. I told Stacy that I would come over and help her go through Dad's stuff." Sarah began to walk back towards the end of her house to her bedroom.

"You want me to come with?"

"No, thanks though Mitch, I really do appreciate it. I just need to go and do this on my own."

"Well if you need anything you just give me a shout."

"I will."

"I'll call you later, okay?"

"Okay, thanks again for everything Mitch, you're a great friend." Mitch just smiled and turned around and left Sarah's house shutting the door on his way out.

Sarah went into her room, changed her clothes and headed over to Stacy's house. Once there, Stacy and Sarah spent about an hour talking about Harold. Sarah told her some stories of when she was growing up and Stacy talked about some of the things the two of them had done together.

"I want to give you and your brother some of your father's personal belongings. But I'm not really sure what you want." Stacy and Sarah were now walking to the back of the house to Harold's den.

The two went in and found the place to be a mess. There were papers, books, and magazines all over the place.

"He wasn't very clean was he?" Sarah asked pushing some of the papers away with her right foot.

"For the most part, yes. But this was his room where he could do as he pleased. You and Raymond should just go through this room and take what you like."

"What about you?"

"I've got plenty of things that he has given me. Oh, and please take all of his guns, I can't stand those things."

"Why?"

"They scare me," Stacy said looking towards the far end of the room where all of his guns were proudly displayed in his gun case. It was the same gun case that he had back when Raymond and Sarah were growing up.

"Don't worry, I'll get Andy to come over and move those to my house today. He really loved those guns," Sarah said.

Sarah ended up spending most of the morning and afternoon at Stacy's house going through her father's den. Every once in awhile Sarah would come out of the room holding some item and asking Stacy what it was. That would get Stacy going off on another story which would trigger some memory for Sarah, which she would then tell.

"I'm going to run home, but I'll be back with Andy and we'll move Dad's gun case."

"Okay, I'll be here."

"Do you have any plans for dinner tonight?" Sarah asked.

"No," Stacy answered thinking about Harold's favorite dish.

"Well why don't you have dinner with Andy, Beth and I tonight."

"I would like that."

"Great. Well I'll figure out at a time and let you know when I get back."

"Okay."

Sarah left the house and went immediately to hers. Once inside she called Andy.

"Hello?"

"Hi, it's me."

"Oh sweetie, I'm so sorry to hear about your dad. Are you okay?"

"I'm hanging in there. I've actually been spending some time with Stacy, dad's girlfriend."

"That's where've you been. I've been trying to get a hold of you all day."

"Yeah. But hey, is there any way you can meet me over at her house. She didn't like dad's guns very much so I'm going to bring them back here. I just need your truck to move it in."

"Yeah, no problem. I'm going to have to call a few people because that thing is going to be heavy."

"Thanks Andy. Oh, and before I forget. I've invited Stacy to dinner with us tonight. You know she really isn't all that bad."

"Oh, okay."

"Good. I'm going to call Beth too, and have her come."

"What?" Andy cleared his throat. "Why are you going to invite Beth?"

"Why wouldn't I? She's family, and in a way so is Stacy."

"Well yeah, but I thought you said she and Raymond where going through some rough times and Beth was getting a divorce?"

"Wait a minute Andy, I never told you that."

"Sure you did, you told me last nig...oh, um never mind."

"No, not never mind. Andy, who told you that?"

"Told me what?"

"Andy quit being stupid. Now who the hell said that?

"I just heard it from...some guys down at Web's last night."

Sarah began to think that Andy's voice sounded a little bit shaky. It also seemed like he was choosing his words carefully like he had something to hide from her. "Oh okay, well meet me at Stacy's in about thirty minutes."

"I will, bye Sarah."

"Bye." Sarah had a bad feeling in her stomach and she knew that it would have something to do with Beth. But what could it be? Sarah decided to go ahead and call Beth to invite her over.

Sarah listened to the phone ring on the other end of the line and remembered that she had not told Raymond about running into Beth at the courthouse, in fact she had completely forgot. A rage of furry came over her and Sarah had a quick change of heart. Just as she was about to hang up Beth answered the phone.

"Hello. Hello?"

"Beth?"

"Hi Sarah. Oh Sarah, Raymond told me about your father. I'm so sorry."

"Thanks."

"How are you doing, is there anything I can do for you?"

"No, I'm okay." Sarah couldn't tell if Beth was being sincere or not. She decided to go ahead and invite her and mention to her that Andy was going to be there. See if she could get any sort of response from her. "So, I'm having a few people over tonight for dinner. It's going to be Stacy, dad's girlfriend and me. Would you like to join us?"

"Oh Sarah, I'd love to. What time?"

"I was thinking around seven."

"Great. Would you like for me to bring anything?"

"That would be nice. Would you mind bringing a salad for four?"

"Sure. But you mean three right?"

"Oh no, sorry I forgot to tell you. Andy is going to be there tonight."

"No problem, I can take care of it." That wasn't the response the Sarah had been looking for. "So I'll see you at seven."

"Alright see you then." Sarah began to think that maybe this whole time she had been over reacting. Once again, she had to remind herself that she wouldn't get this way. Sarah already had too much drama in her life.

When Sarah got back to Stacy's house she could see that her father's gun case was already in the back of Andy's truck. Sarah walked in and found her in the kitchen.

"I'm back."

"Sarah, I can't make it tonight."

"What? Why?"

"I just can't bring myself to leave the house. I just want to be alone." Stacy said.

"Are you sure? Do you want be to bring you some supper?"

"No, I'm fine. Look, maybe after the funeral. I just can't right now."

"I understand," Sarah said as she went up and gave Stacy a hug. "If there is anything, anything, you let me know."

"I will."

Sarah walked outside and noticed that Andy's truck was already gone. She assumed that he had already gone back to her house to unload the gun case. She thought that it was odd that he had completely avoided her. He had to have heard her voice from inside the house. But she supposed in some weird chance that he hadn't. So Sarah began to walk home.

Once Sarah made it, she saw Andy's truck sitting right outside her house. She noticed that the gun case wasn't in there. Sarah crossed the street and walked up the walkway that led to her front door. Her front door was left open so she walked right in. She saw the gun case put up against one of the walls in her living room. She thought how horrible it looked and had immediately decided that it was going to go to Raymond when he got back in town.

Sarah turned her head in the living room trying to see where Andy was. She heard a flushing sound coming from the bathroom and then out walked Andy.

"Oh, hey," Andy said.

"Hi."

"Is it okay there?" Andy asked pointing to the gun case.

"Yeah until Raymond makes it back into town. I'm just going to let him have it."

"Oh okay. Well I really need to get going."

"Alright. I'm calling off the dinner tonight. Stacy just wasn't ready and now that I think about it, I don't think that I am either."

"Okay, well maybe some other time. Did you tell Beth?"

"No, not yet."

"Well I'll call her for you if you want. You seem like you're a little tired."

She was. Sarah hadn't realized it, but she hadn't gotten much sleep from the night before. And now she felt the whole world on her shoulders and just wanted nothing more than to go to bed.

"I am feeling a little bit sleepy. I think I will try to take a short nap."

"Well I'll call you later okay, Hun?" Andy went and gave Sarah a kiss. "Bye."

"Good bye."

Andy showed himself out while Sarah went back into her bedroom and lay down on her bed. Lying on her back, Sarah stared at the ceiling. It seemed like the sleep had left her body. She didn't feel like getting back up and doing something, so she just thought. She tried to think of her childhood and remember all the good times that she had with her father. But only a few came to mind.

As she continued to think, she thought about how her father had left his family, her mother killing herself, her father coming back home and turning into an alcoholic, and having to live with her brother. It was at this moment that Sarah realized that she had such a horrible childhood. Sarah now thought of herself as a hard woman and came to the conclusion it was because of the life that she had to live.

Tears again filled her eyes. She felt alone in that bed. It seemed like her life was falling apart all around her. As the evening went on Sarah could hear the wind outside her bedroom window start to pick up. Every once in awhile, she would see her room brighten from the lightning followed seconds later by a rolling clap of thunder.

Sarah woke up the next morning and looked out her window. She saw nothing but puddles of water all over her yard. She glanced at the clock hanging on her bedroom wall, it said 10:45. Sarah still felt tired but knew that she shouldn't go back to bed. Instead, she put on some clothes and headed out the door.

The air felt muggy and the smell of it said that another down pour would soon be coming. Sarah felt like a nice walk would be just the thing she needed. So she walked down Main Street and was surprised to see it mostly empty. Usually there were many people out and about getting things done in front of their shops, but today was not the case. After walking a while she ended up at the other end of town. Across the street from her was Web's and she noticed the lights inside were on.

"That's odd," Sarah said to herself. Sarah knew that John usually didn't come into work until after one. So Sarah ran across the street to see what was going on. There were many puddles and Sarah tried to jump over them so that they wouldn't splash back on her. Once on the other side, Sarah walked up to the door of Web's and turned the doorknob. To her shock it was unlocked.

"Hello?" Sarah called out as she stepped inside.

"Sarah, is that you?" A female voice called out from the back.

"Yeah it's me, Becky." Becky came from the back of the bar, her sweat pants completely soaked. "Becky, what happened?"

"That damn storm, that's what happened. We've got a hole in the roof and the back is just flooded. Oh listen to me, God Sarah, I'm sorry. How are you doing?"

"I'm getting by. It's weird you know. I never really spent time with my dad during the last few years of his life and frankly I really didn't miss him all that much. But now that he's gone, it scares the hell out of me."

"Of course it does Sarah. You may not have been around him all that much, but you always knew that he was there."

"I know." Sarah looked down at her feet not really knowing what to say next. She didn't even know how she ended up at Web's in the first place. "So are you and John going to be able to come to the funeral?"

"Of course sweetie, we want to be there for you."

"I don't know what I would do without you guys. I mean other than Andy, Beth, and Raymond you two are like family."

Becky began to look and feel uncomfortable. She knew that Sarah didn't know a lot about what was going on behind her back. She wanted nothing more than to take Sarah in her arms and give her a great big hug and tell her everything that she had heard. Becky knew that Sarah deserved better then Andy and also wanted nothing more than to get Beth out of Sumertown once and for all. Becky must have had a look on her face that said something was wrong because Sarah was quick to pick it up.

"Becky?"

"Yeah."

"What's going on?"

"Nothing," Becky replied looking down at her feet. "I'm just worried about getting this mess cleaned up here, that's all," Becky said as she turned around and started to walk to the back of the bar.

Sarah took a few quick steps to get to Becky and gently grabbed her by her arm.

"Now isn't the time, Sarah. You've been through enough this week," Becky replied as she turned to face Sarah with a single tear running down her left cheek. "After the funeral you and I need to have a long talk." Becky again turned around to start towards the back but Sarah's hand was still on Becky's arm. Sarah gave a slight pull.

"No. We need to talk now," Sarah said with Becky's back facing her. Sarah let go of her arm. Becky stood there for a moment thinking how exactly to start this off. How do you tell your best friend something like this?

"Why don't we sit down," Becky said as she walked over to the closest table. Sarah followed behind her, her heart beating so fast it felt as if it was about to burst out of her chest. The two of them sat down sitting across from each other. "You know that I wouldn't be telling you something like this if I didn't actually believe it myself?"

"I know," Sarah replied while nodding her head.

"Did you know that Beth comes in here once a week?"

Sarah shook her head no. In fact she was a little shocked. Except for a few times when Beth had first moved to Sumertown, Sarah could not recall a time that she had seen her in Web's. "Are we usually busy when she comes in?" Sarah questioned.

"Oh yeah, we're busy. But here's the thing, she only comes in whenever you aren't working." Sarah sat up right in her chair. She definitely did not like the way this was going and already she could feel her face become warm from her temper. "And usually when she comes in here she has a few drinks, gets pretty much drunk off her ass, and leaves with some guy."

"I can't believe this," Sarah said shaking her head as she began to cry. "Raymond has always been so good to her. I mean, sure he's gone a lot, but that is only because she likes to spend money. And you've got to bring in the money to be able to spend it."

"Sarah you don't have to make excuses for Raymond. Everybody in this town knows how great of a person he is and how he can do so much better than Beth, but..." Becky cleared her throat and paused. She saw how Sarah was taking the news of the affair, but the worst was still yet to come.

"But what?" Sarah asked as she wiped the tears from her face with her hand.

"Most of the time she always leaves with the same guy. Now granted, I don't know what they are or aren't doing when they leave here, and truthfully I don't care to know." Becky stopped again to see if Sarah knew where this was going. She couldn't really tell if she had been able to figure it out, or if she was still upset from finding out about Beth. "But Sarah here's the thing. This...guy, he's in here all the time. And yea, when he gets to drinking too much he starts to say stuff, you know, about him and Beth. I don't know if it's just the alcohol talking, but if you ask me, everything that he says is true. I see how they interact with each other and it makes me sick to my stomach because I always think of you."

"Why would you think of me? Wouldn't it be Raymond that you would be more concerned about?" It was becoming more obvious to Becky that Sarah didn't understand where exactly this was going. Becky looked away shaking her head. "Oh my God," Sarah said, bringing her hand up to her mouth in shock. "It all makes sense now. I mean, he hasn't really been around all that much these last few months, and I always thought that it was because of me and, no. It's because he's been with Beth. I can't believe Mitch would do something like this." Sarah said as she quickly stood up from the table.

"What are you talking about?" Beth asked as she also stood up.

"Ever since I've been with Andy, he's been distancing himself from me. That must have been around the time that he started this whole affair."

"Dammit, Sarah, listen to yourself. It's not Mitch, he would never be so selfish. And you know damn well that he would never do anything that would hurt you." At that time the door opened and John walked in carrying a large box. "Sarah, Beth's been having an affair with Andy."

"What?" Sarah said taking a few steps back from the table.

"What the hell are you doing?" John asked dropping the box and walking over towards them. "What has gotten into you?"

"She wanted to know," Becky snapped to her husband.

"Oh I see, she just came in here and asked who her sister-in-law was screwing?"

Becky and John continued to argue back and forth with each other. Sarah stood behind them lost in her own little world. She could see the two of them right in front of her but couldn't hear a single thing that they were saying. She suddenly felt lightheaded and went to reach for a chair that was beside her. But as she reached for it she began to break out in a heavy sweat and it seemed that the chair was moving away from her. Standing in place she reached further and further for the chair but couldn't seem to grasp it.

"Sarah. Sarah what are you doing?" John asked looking over Becky's shoulder toward Sarah.

"I'm trying to get that chair," Sarah said still reaching. She sounded like she was out of breath, like she had just finished running a marathon.

Becky turned around to see just how pale Sarah was. "Sarah, I'll get that," Becky said going over and getting her the

113

chair. She helped Sarah sit down and noticed just how unstable she was. "John get a wet towel, she's burning up."

"How could this happen? Why would he, and she, why would they do this to us?"

"Sarah just calm down. Now like I said I don't really know if all this is true but after everything that I…"

Becky continued to explain all the things that she had observed between Andy and Beth, but Sarah had already faded her out. All Sarah could do now was think how stupid she was for not noticing any of this sooner. Flash backs began to fill her head, remembering all the times that she had asked Andy to do something with her and him saying that he was busy doing something else. Just that thought alone filled her head with even more. How many times was he busy doing something else when in truth he was doing Beth? She remembered that just recently the mention of Beth's name would send the look of guilt across his face. Sure, she had thought that it was odd but never in her wildest dreams did she actually think that Andy would go and do something like this to her. They loved each other, they were supposed to be getting married. The more that she thought it about it the angrier she got. In fact, her shocked broken heart was quickly turning bitter and she wanted nothing more than to get revenge on both of them.

As Becky continued to talk to Sarah, John had come over with a wet towel. Sarah felt him lifting her legs and resting them on another chair while Becky was patting Sarah's forehead with the towel. During all this she still had not been paying much attention to either one of them. She had only one thing on her mind right now and that was how she was going to handle all of this.

"Sarah?" Becky asked looking at her. "Sarah have you heard anything that I have just said to you?"

"They're going to pay for this Becky, both of them."

"Now Sarah don't go do anything stupid, you're smarter than that," John said. "Are you going to tell Raymond?"

"Of course I am! Why wouldn't I? Do you honestly think that I want him to be married to that damn slut any longer than what he has to be? I'm going to wait until he comes back for Dad's funeral. He doesn't need to find out before then, do y'all understand?" Sarah asked looking back and forth between the two of them. They both nodded their heads in agreement. "I don't need him rushing back here in rage and end up wrecking. I'm already having to bury one family member, I don't need to do a second one." Sarah's face was now extremely red. "I just need to leave and walk this frustration off," she said getting up from her chair. Both John and Becky also stood up.

"Honey, is there anything at all that we can do for you?" Becky asked reaching her arm out to rub Sarah's shoulder.

"No. Look, I also don't want either one of you to say anything to Andy or Beth. I'm going to have to deal with this in my own way, that includes confronting the two of them."

"We won't Sarah, if that's what you want," John replied.

"It is. There is just one thing I need to know from the both of you," Sarah said looking back and forth between their eyes. "If the two of you knew this was going on, why wouldn't you tell Raymond or me?"

John looked down at his feet, feeling too embarrassed to look Sarah in the face. Sure he wanted to tell both of them what was going on, but all this time he had felt that it wasn't really his place to do so. That is, he had felt that way up until now.

Becky, on the other hand, wasn't feeling so much that she should tell Raymond, but the whole time she had been dying to tell Sarah. It ate her up inside that she wasn't able to tell her. Back when the affair had first started, both John and Becky had been aware of it. But John had convinced his wife that this was something that Raymond and Sarah were going to have to find out for themselves. Now Becky was crying. She knew how betrayed Sarah must have felt by them not telling her.

"I simply wish the two of you would have just told us." Sarah said again as she turned and started walking towards the door.

Becky went to go catch up to her but John had put his arm out to stop her and shook his head back and forth. "She needs to be alone," he said as they both watched Sarah walk out of the bar.

Sarah walked outside and her breath was immediately taken away by the humidity in the air. Off in the distance, she could see dark clouds coming and knew that a thunderstorm was quickly approaching.

When Sarah got home, she tried to put her mind at ease. Today she and Stacy would be going over to the funeral home to make sure that every last detail was in order for the funeral tomorrow. This made it all seem so final. The one thing that she had regretted was that it took a tragedy to bring her and Stacy closer together. Sarah sat in her living room staring off into space.

Without even realizing it, she found herself looking at her father's gun case sitting in the one corner. She got up from her couch, crossed the room and was now standing directly in front of the case. It was actually a beautiful piece. Sarah wondered what it was like, how it felt to shoot a gun, or even hold one for that matter. With curiosity getting the better of her, she opened up the glass front, revealing her father's guns. Standing upright were three riffles. On both ends were spots to put four pistols on each side. These sides were only filled with two pistols each.

Sarah slowly reached her arm towards the smallest gun. She wanted to feel the weight of it in her hand. She grabbed the gun and slowly lifted it from its holder. It was a small six-barrel pistol. The steel felt very cool in her hands. As she brought the gun closer to her, she was shocked at how heavy it was.

As she stood there holding that gun a rush of adrenaline ran throughout her body. She felt like she was in charge. Holding the gun in her right hand she slowly raised her arm extending it out and pointing the gun straight ahead. She tilted her head slightly to the right and closed her left eye. She concentrated down her arm and focused on the sight at the end of the gun. It was at that moment she knew exactly what needed to be done. Sarah gave a little smile; she had it figured out. At that moment there was a bright flash outside her living room window followed by an extremely loud boom of thunder.

"Shit," Sarah said in fright. Without realizing it, she dropped the gun and fell to the floor the same time the gun did. Sarah laid there in a fetal position, her knees tucked into her chest and her arms over her head. She lay there for a moment not moving. She opened her eyes and saw the gun lying in front of her. It wasn't loaded.

Sarah let out a sigh and slowly got to her feet. She was afraid that the gun would have discharged since she had dropped it. Sarah bent down to pick up the gun, looked it over one last time and put it back in the gun case.

Outside she could hear the sound of rain hitting her window with an occasional flash of lightning. She still had to go to the funeral home with Stacy later on that afternoon. But what would tomorrow bring. She was going to have to face both Andy and Beth and the thought of that infuriated her. Also, she still needed to find a way to tell Raymond. That was probably going to be the hardest part of it all.

Sarah grabbed her umbrella and headed out the door. It was now starting to rain a bit harder than earlier. With her umbrella open, Sarah quickly ran down the street to her father's house. About half way there, a gust of wind caught Sarah's umbrella and flipped it inside out. Sarah stood there fumbling with it for a second getting it to turn right side in, and back on her way.

She got to the house and saw that the front door was open. Sarah closed her umbrella and left it resting beside the door and walked into the house.

"Stacy?" Sarah called out.

"I'm in the kitchen," she heard a voice call back. Sarah went back into the kitchen and found Stacy sitting at the table drinking a cup of tea. "Would you like anything to drink?" Stacy asked Sarah. Her voice and face were expressionless. Stacy just sat at the table looking off into space.

"No, I'm okay. Look Stacy, we should really get going."

"You're right. Let me go get my jacket," and with still no expression, Stacy arose from the table and walked back towards the front of the house. Sarah followed close behind her. She felt so sorry for her. Here was this woman whose only person in her life was her father, and now she must have felt alone.

Stacy grabbed her jacket from the back of the couch and put it on. She proceeded to the front door and took her keys off the table by the door and handed them to Sarah. Without saying a word Sarah took the keys from Stacy and the two women left the house, got into Stacy's car and drove to the funeral home.

The two met with the funeral home director and went over which songs they wanted to be played, which bible scriptures were going to be read and who would be speaking. Sarah ended up doing most of the talking. Every now and then, when asked a question, Sarah would answer and then look over at Stacy and ask, "Is that going to be okay?" Stacy would only respond with a slight nod of the head.

At the end, the director asked if they would like to view the body. Sarah passed because she remembered how bad her father looked when he was in the hospital and didn't want to see him like that ever again. Stacy on the other hand immediately jumped from her seat. She wanted to see him. Sarah saw Stacy follow the funeral director behind a closed door. Seconds later she could hear Stacy screaming and sobbing hysterically. Sarah got up from her seat to see what was wrong about the same time the director came from behind the door.

"What's going on in there?" she asked him.

"This is actually common." He replied. "A lot of people have a hard time coping with the death of a loved one. Some people don't think that it is possible that they could even be gone. But when they see them in a coffin the reality hits them and hits them hard. Then all those emotions that they had either been holding back or didn't know how to express come flooding out."

"Well, is she going to be okay?"

"In time, yes. She just needs to mourn."

Sarah had decided to leave Stacy there. She gave the funeral director the keys to Stacy's car and asked that he make sure she got home all right. She had a feeling that Stacy was going to be there for awhile. It wasn't until that moment that she realized Stacy had put her feelings aside for her. She stayed away and let Sarah have the last moments of her father's life with her. She simply stood in the back of the room and had not had her chance to say good bye.

Sarah walked outside into the pouring rain. She opened her umbrella and started to walk home. She knew that Raymond would be home probably sometime late this afternoon. She had decided to not tell him until after the funeral.

After walking two blocks a truck pulled up beside her and honked its horn. Sarah looked over and the drivers' side window was being rolled down.

"Need a lift?" It was Mitch.

"Yea," Sarah said as she walked around the front end of his truck and climbed in the passenger side.

"Man, we ain't seen rain like this for a long time. We are probably going to see some flooding."

"Probably," Sarah replied looking out her window.

"What's wrong?"

"What do you mean?" Sarah asked looking over at him.

"You're just more quiet than usual. Is it because of your dad? Damn I'm sorry, I shouldn't have even brought that up."

"No, it's not that. I've just got a lot going on, that's all."

"When's Raymond getting home?"

"Sometime later today. Are you coming to the funeral tomorrow?"

"Of course I am. I want to be there for the two of you. Y'all are like family to me, you know that."

"I know."

The rest of the short ride went by in silence. When Mitch pulled up in front of Sarah's house she invited him in for some lunch and he agreed. They both ran to the front door as Sarah fumbled to get the key in the door. Once inside, Sarah and Mitch walked back to the kitchen.

"You want a turkey or ham sandwich?" She asked.

"How about a little bit of both?"

"Sure. Hey can I ask you something?" Sarah asked as she was reaching into the refrigerator.

"Shoot."

"I found something out today and I was wondering if you had heard anything, or knew about this."

"Okay," Mitch replied.

"I was at Web's this morning," at that moment the phone rang. "Hold on a second." Sarah walked back into the living room where the phone rang again. "Hello?"

"Hey Sis," it was Raymond.

"Hi Raymond. Where are you?"

"Bad news, I'm still in Candletop," Raymond replied.

"Okay. So when are you planning on getting here?"

"Look Sarah, the roads are completely flooded up here. Everyone that I have been talking to say that this is probably the worst storm they've ever seen. I don't even know when I'm going to be able to get out of here."

"What!" Sarah yelled.

Mitch looked over at her and mouthed, "What's wrong?" But Sarah simply waved him off.

"Sarah, if there was a way I could get home trust me, I would do it. Right now I'm looking at other ways of getting around some of the roads that are completely covered with water. I'm sorry, but I don't think that I'm going to be able to make it to the funeral tomorrow."

"This is so typical of you, Raymond. You know if you didn't want to be here for Dad's funeral you should have just said something to me the other day."

"Look Sarah, if there was a way I would be..."

Sarah had already heard enough and slammed the phone down. "Can you believe him? He isn't going to be here for Dad's funeral. He's putting the blame on this damn weather."

"Sarah the weather is bad, and you know that if Raymond says that he can't be here because of the weather then he's telling the truth," Mitch said trying to reassure Sarah.

"No, he's just acting like a kid. He never got along with Dad so this is his one last way of getting even with him. I hate him. I absolutely hate him for doing this to me," Sarah said. Her face was deep purple and her eyes began to glass over with tears. Mitch had decided not to disagree with Sarah. He knew that once she had her mind set on something, then there was no changing it. "Why? I just don't understand why," Sarah said pacing back and forth in the kitchen. "He needs to be here, Mitch. I mean the whole thing with Beth and Andy," Sarah threw her arms up into the air and again started to cry. She looked over at Mitch who had guilt written all over his face. The second the two made eye contact he was quick to look away. "Why?" She whimpered. "Why didn't you tell me, Mitch? We've been best friends for how long? And you knew, didn't you?" Mitch still wouldn't look up at Sarah. "Mitch, answer me."

"What was I supposed to do, Sarah? Was I supposed to just come out and tell you?"

"Of course. You knew what he was doing behind my back, and Raymond's also. I can understand why everybody else in town wouldn't say anything to either one of us. But you, I just can't believe it. How dare you keep something like this from us."

"How dare...how dare I? Look Sarah the only reason that I didn't tell you or Raymond what I knew is because you are both stubborn asses."

"WHAT?" Sarah snapped back.

"That's right, stubborn asses. Raymond and I tried telling you what Andy was like when you first started going out

123

with him. But would you listen, hell no. You went into one of those pissy moods of yours like the whole world was against you. And your brother is just as bad. Why do you think I came over that night that Raymond showed back up in town with Beth?" Sarah didn't answer. "It's because he and I got into it. I asked him how could he be so stupid as to end up with her. Let's see, Beth comes into town, I try to hook up with her. Andy comes in and takes her away. It's no surprise that they would both cheat on you, and truthfully it's no surprise that they end up back together. So the way I see it, y'all both got what was coming to you." Mitch just stood there waiting for a response from Sarah.

"Get out. Get out of my house you son of a bitch. How dare you talk to me like this?"

"Look, Sarah, you asked me..."

"I said get out," Sarah turned around and found a coffee mug in the sink. She picked it up, turned back around and threw it at Mitch. Mitch was quick enough to duck so the cup wouldn't hit him. The coffee mug hit the wall behind him and broke into several large pieces.

"I'm out of here." Mitch said, as he quickly made his way to the front door to leave.

Sarah sat down on the kitchen floor. At this moment in her life she didn't know if there was a single person that she could trust. For months the entire town knew this deep dirty secret and nobody had bothered to tell her. They were more interested in gossiping then they were in telling her the truth.

* * * * * * * * *

"Till this day, I can't think of a time that I had ever been so hurt in all my life," Sarah continued while lying in her hospital bed. It was now just past five. A nurse had already

124

brought her in her supper but Sarah didn't have much of an appetite, so the tray of food sat on the windowsill as she continued with her story.

"That evening, I found myself once again in front of Dad's gun case. I had never shot a gun before, and up until that moment I never had any intentions of doing so either. I don't know why I did it. It could have been all the rage that was brewing up inside of me, or merely the rush of the feeling of having so much power by holding that gun in my hand. Whatever it was, I opened the chamber of the pistol to find it empty. It didn't take me long to find the bullets. Once I had though, I carefully placed each bullet into the chamber until all six spots were full."

Suspicion began to grow with her listeners as Sarah continued with her story. "I took that gun and put it in my purse. I just had to see what it felt to like to shoot one of those things. I was in a way, very excited. So with my purse in hand I left my house, got into my car and drove outside of Sumertown.

"I didn't remember much when I was driving and had no idea where I was going. Before I knew it I found myself turning into the old grown-over driveway that led to our old house. I sat in the car with the engine running and stared at the house. It had been years since Dad lived there and nobody had occupied it since. It looked like a dark shadow, a forgotten memory.

"I turned the car off, reached into my purse and pulled out the gun. I could feel my heart racing as I proceeded to open the car door and get out. I started to look around in all directions, I just knew that somebody was going to see me out there and I was going to get caught. But the weather was pretty much keeping everybody indoors.

"Once I had myself convinced that nobody was in the area I started to walk towards the back end of the house. The ground was extremely soft from all the rain we had been having. Each step that I took, my foot would slip and slosh in the muddy ground. I had to be extremely careful because the last thing that I wanted to do was fall while holding the gun.

"Once I made it to the back yard I just stood there. Those large oak trees still towered high above, just the way I remembered from when I was growing up. I walked towards the back porch. It was in horrible shape. The stairs leading up to it had nearly rotted away. And the porch itself was covered in mold. I had thought about going inside but decided not to. Besides if I had, I would have probably fallen through the floor.

"With the gun still in my hand I turned my back to the house and faced the back yard. For the first time in my life I was going to shoot a gun. I slowly extended my right arm till it was stretched out in front of me. I tilted my head to the right and looked down my arm towards the end of the gun. I closed my left eye and used the little pin at the end of the gun and fixed it on one of the trees. I stood there for just a moment. Then as if I had already done it a hundred times before, I pulled back on the hammer with my thumb and brought my finger up to the trigger and slowly pulled on it."

* * * * * * * * *

The gun fired loudly and Sarah's right arm went flying upward. "Oh my God," Sarah said as her arm fell back down to her side, the gun still in her right hand. She gently bent down and set the gun on the grass. She had a terrible ringing in her ears now and she began rubbing them hoping that would make it stop.

Sarah looked around her still hoping that there wasn't anyone nearby. She was shocked by how loud the gun was. She couldn't remember the last time she had heard one being shot. She knew it had to have been sometime after her dad had come back, but couldn't remember how long it had been.

After standing in the same spot for a few moments she looked toward the large oak trees to see if she had actually hit one. She saw nothing. So Sarah decided to try again. She picked the gun up off the ground and again extended her right arm straight out in front of her. This time Sarah brought her left arm up and grabbed the bottom of the pistol. She made sure that both of her arms were stretched out firmly in front of her. Again she tilted her head to the right and stared at the pin at the end of the gun. She focused it on another tree, pulled back on the hammer, brought her finger to the trigger and pulled it again. Again the pistol fired and Sarah's arm slightly pushed upward. Just ahead of her she saw the bark of one of the trees splinter.

"I hit it?" Sarah asked herself with a half laugh as if she was shocked she was actually able to do it. "I can't believe I hit it."

Sarah walked up to the tree that she had hit and looked where the bullet had gone into the bark. She turned back around to try and guess just how far away she had been standing. She had guessed it to be about thirty feet, not very far, but further away from where she would actually be.

Sarah walked back to the spot where she had just been standing and again shot the gun. Just like it had just done she saw the bark splinter. She fired three more shots at the same tree with each of the bullets striking it.

Sarah now felt extremely confident in herself, almost too confident. She began to walk back around to the front of the house towards her car. Just before she opened her car door, she raised her gun straight up into the air and fired the remaining shot. Then with a smirk on her face, Sarah got back into her car and headed back into town.

That night Sarah was at home by herself. She had taken the phone off the hook and kept almost all the lights in her house off. She did not want to be disturbed while she was trying to come up with a plan. Sarah sat in her bathroom on the edge of the tub. It was the only room in her house that didn't have a window so she was able to keep the light on. With a pad of paper on her lap and a pencil in her right hand she began to scribble notes. She knew that both Andy and Beth would have to pay for what they had done. The two of them had caused a great deal of embarrassment to her and Raymond, and Sarah wasn't the type to just let it go. She had to make sure that neither of them would ever have the chance to do anything like this again. Sarah knew that the only way to get this accomplished was to kill them both.

She thought the best way to do this was when they were together, and she wanted to get it done as soon as possible. This meant two things. One, she had to know when they would be with each other, and two, she couldn't let on that she knew anything. She knew that the element of surprise would be priceless.

Once Sarah was satisfied with everything that she had come up with, she figured that she should go ahead and get some sleep. She walked back to her father's gun cabinet, reloaded the pistol that she had fired earlier and put the gun back into her purse. It was now very late, and tomorrow was going to be a long day.

The next morning Sarah awoke to someone pounding on her front door. She sluggishly pulled herself out of bed and walked to the front of her house. The person at the door continued to pound on it.

"I'm coming," Sarah called out as she reached for the lock. The knocking stopped as she unlocked and opened her door. There stood Becky, her eyes extremely puffy, standing in the rain. "What do you need?" Sarah asked her. She was still upset with her and John for keeping their secret from her and Raymond.

"Sarah, you know that John and I never wanted to hurt you," her eyes began to fill with tears again.

Sarah felt sorry for her. It was more than obvious how much this had been bothering her. "Get in here before you catch a cold." Becky walked into Sarah's house and followed her to the kitchen. "Sit down and I'll get you a towel and something warm to drink," Sarah said as she walked down the hallway to the closet.

Becky sat there wondering what to say. She noticed a dent on the wall above the table and followed it down to the floor to see the shattered mug. As Sarah walked back from the closet, she noticed Becky staring at it.

"I was a little upset last night," she said as she handed Becky the towel. "Raymond called and said that he wasn't going to be here for dad's funeral." Sarah didn't want to tell Becky what had really happened, she was too embarrassed.

"Sarah, I'm sorry," Becky said still just holding the towel.

"Look, it's over," Sarah was now in the kitchen starting to boil water for some tea. "And I'm sure that you and John had your reasons for not telling me. Besides, I'm not really the easiest person to tell something like this to." Sarah started to think how she had talked to and treated Mitchell and knew that she would need to call him and apologize. "Seriously Becky, don't worry about it. I'm not upset with the two of you, just at the situation."

"Have you talked to them yet?" Becky asked.

"No," Sarah answered shaking her head back and forth. "I will though. I just don't think that today is the day to do it." The kettle on the stove was now whistling. Sarah had a terrible feeling in her gut. She knew that she couldn't actually kill someone. But in the same breath she thought of Andy and Beth together and her guilt turned to hate.

"Sarah, the water's done."

Sarah blinked a couple of times and noticed the steam coming out of the pot. She turned the gas off to the stove and poured the hot water into two cups with tea bags already in them.

Sarah took the two cups back to the table and the two of them sat there in silence as they sipped their tea. It was a little awkward for the both of them but neither one of them knew what to say to the other.

"Look, I really need to get going," Becky said as she set her cup on the table and stood up. "Did you want to come to the funeral with John and me?"

"No, thanks though." Sarah stood up and walked Becky to the door. "Look, I would really appreciate it if you didn't say anything to anybody about this, I just need to deal with it in my own way."

"I won't," Becky replied as she handed the towel back to Sarah. "I'll see you later on." Sarah shut the door and walked back into her bedroom.

It was just past ten and Sarah was sitting on her couch putting her makeup on when there was a knock at the door. Sarah closed her compact and got up from the couch. She looked through the peephole and saw Andy standing at the door. Sarah stepped back and took in a deep breath. There was another knock at the door and Sarah began to feel her face become warm. She needed to keep control over herself as not let on that she knew about him and Beth.

"Sarah, are ya home?" Andy called out from the other side of the door.

"Give me a second," she replied with her hand on the doorknob. With one last breath she turned the doorknob and opened the door. "Hey, Andy."

"Good morning," Andy said as he reached in and gave her a kiss on the lips. Sarah returned the kiss with both her arms at her sides. She couldn't believe that he was acting as if he had done nothing wrong. "You almost ready?"

"Yea I just got done with my makeup. Let me go slip my dress on and then we can get going," Sarah replied as she began to make her way to her room.

"Do you need any help?" Andy asked as he began to follow her back.

Sarah turned around and looked at him, she was even more pissed. "Andy, I'm about to bury my father, do you really think that now is the time?" Without giving him the chance to answer she turned back around, went into her room, and shut the door. She was letting her frustration over the situation get the better of her, and the last thing that she wanted was for Andy to figure out what Sarah knew.

Sarah took the dress off her bed that she had laid out earlier and put it on. Looking in the mirror that hung on the wall in her room, she brushed her hands down her black dress, checked to make sure that her hair was okay, and proceeded back into the living room where Andy stood there waiting for her.

"Sarah, I'm sorry, I didn't mean anything by that. I couldn't even begin to think what you are going through right now."

He was right, Sarah had thought to herself. He had absolutely no idea what was going on in her mind.

"It's okay, Andy, I shouldn't have snapped at you. It's not like you did anything wrong, you were just being yourself," Sarah said as she walked up to him and gave him a hug. Andy wrapped his arms around her and rubbed her back, not knowing how to take the comment that Sarah had just made to him. "We should probably get over to the funeral home," Sarah said as she pulled away from his embrace.

The funeral home was just a short distance from Sarah's home and the ride over had been one with no conversation. Once they got there, Andy parked the car and then both he and Sarah got out and began to walk into the building. Andy had wrapped his arm around Sarah's shoulder. She thought to herself how good that felt to her. She began to second-guess everything that she had heard. If he really loved her that much how could any of those rumors be true? In what was one of the darkest moments in her life he was there for her.

Once inside the building, Sarah had noticed that there were more people there for her father's funeral then she had expected. A lot of the people were up and talking with some of the other guests, some had already taken their seats. Then up at the front, she saw her father's casket and standing there with a tissue held to her face was Stacy.

With his arm still around Sarah, Andy had started to talk with one of the guests. "I'm going to go talk to Stacy," Sarah said as she walked away.

"Okay Hun," Andy replied.

As Sarah walked up the isle between the chairs, she saw some of the people look up at her. Many of them started to whisper things to the person that was sitting next to them, others offered their condolences as she passed them. Sarah's eyes began to fill with tears as she approached the casket. For a moment she stood right behind Stacy staring at her father.

He looked like he was sleeping. Sarah couldn't believe that this was going to be the last time she would get to see her father again. She had only wished she could have been a better daughter to him, and have not blocked him out of her life as much as she had done. She didn't know why she had done it. Maybe it was for Raymond. She knew how much he hated him, and maybe in a way to please him she didn't spend the time like she should have when her father was still alive.

Sarah walked closer up to Stacy and placed her right hand gently on her left shoulder. Stacy jumped a little and looked over her shoulder to see a tearful Sarah standing there. Without a word being spoken Stacy turned around and gave Sarah a hug. The two of them stood there for a moment just hugging, the whole time Sarah saw her father's body lying in his casket.

"Where's Raymond?" Stacy asked.

"He's not going to be able to make it," Sarah had completely forgotten about her brother and now felt horrible for the way she had treated him on the phone. "The roads are all covered with water from all the rain."

Stacy again started to tear up and with one arm around her shoulder, Sarah walked her back to the pew so the service could get started. The two of them sat right in the front with Stacy to Sarah's left. Next to Sarah was Andy and next to him was Beth.

"We are here today to remember a great man," the pastor began.

"I can't believe he didn't show up to his own father's funeral," Sarah heard somebody whisper behind her.

133

Sarah turned around to the lady behind her who had been talking. "Do you mind waiting until after I have buried my father to start your gossip?" She sternly asked. The lady simply looked past her without saying a word or even acknowledging the fact that Sarah was speaking to her.

As Sarah was beginning to turn back around, she saw Mitch sitting a few rows back. Her eyes caught his and he gave her a half smile. She felt horrible for the way that she had treated him. Sarah lipped, "I'm sorry," to him, and he nodded his head in acceptance. Sarah then turned back around once again facing her father. She let out a sigh and as she did Andy reached his arm around her and held her.

The service went on for an hour. Several people got up and spoke including Stacy. Sarah had no idea how many people cared for her father and how much of an impact he had actually made on Sumertown.

When the service concluded, everybody went out to the cemetery for the burial. A bagpiper was out there playing Amazing Grace. As his coffin was being lowered, the pastor read several psalms aloud. At the last moment before the casket was out of sight, with a single tear rolling down her cheek, Sarah closed her eyes and saw her father. "I love you, Dad," she whispered. When she opened her eyes, her father had been laid to rest.

After the coffin had been lowered everyone began to walk away. The only people that had remained were Sarah, Stacy, Andy, and Beth. Both Sarah and Stacy needed just a few minutes before accepting the fact that this was the end for a man that they both loved.

Stacy turned around and again saw tears in Sarah's eyes. "Thanks for everything that you have done during this whole thing," she said.

"It's not a problem, don't you worry about it," Sarah replied. "You know that if anything comes up and you need someone to talk to call me, day or night, I don't mind."

"I will, thanks."

The four of them began to walk away from the grave and towards their own cars in the nearby parking lot. Beth got in her car and pulled out of the parking lot as Sarah and Stacy were both unlocking their car doors. Just before Sarah ducked her head to get into the car, Stacy turned around.

"Look Sarah, don't be mad at your brother for not being here today," Stacy said. "Take it from me, life is too short to stay mad at someone. You never know when they will be gone from your life." Sarah simply nodded and watched as Stacy got into her car and started the engine. Sarah then proceeded to get into her own car and reached over to the passenger side door to unlock it to let Andy get in.

Andy got into the car, shut his door, and put his seatbelt on. Sarah started the car and watched from her rearview mirror waiting for Stacy to pull out. Once she had, Sarah put her car into reverse and backed out of her parking spot.

"It was a really nice service," Andy said, finally breaking the silence.

"Yes it was," Sarah replied.

Sarah couldn't stop thinking about what Stacy had just said to her. She was right, life was too short to stay mad at anyone. And the more she thought about it the more she thought it pertained to not only Raymond.

There was no reason for Sarah to stay mad at Becky and John. She had been friends with them for so long, and even though they had suspected Andy and Beth of having an affair with each other, they truly kept it from them because they were trying to be protective.

As for Andy and Beth, they had obviously made their choice that they wanted to be with each other. Sarah knew that she would have to accept that. The only thing that was bothering her was that they were doing it behind hers and Raymond's back. If this was truly the choice that they wanted to make, then they should fess up and tell her and...

"What's the matter? You've hardly said two words to me all day," Andy asked.

"I just have a lot on my mind," she replied. "You wanna go grab some lunch?"

"Sure," Andy replied.

Sarah pulled into the diner and they both went in and ordered their lunch. Andy got a BLT while Sarah ordered the chicken salad. The entire meal was eaten in almost complete silence. Except for the occasional, "This is good," or "Would you hand me the catsup," they simply stared down at the food they ate.

The entire time they sat there, Sarah wanted so badly to just confront Andy and ask him if he was sleeping with Beth. But as soon as she thought she had worked up enough nerve to ask him, her heart would start racing and she would find herself at a loss of words.

"So how was everything?" the waitress asked in a chipper happy voice as she approached their table.

"Just fine, thank you," Sarah answered.

"Good, that's what we like to hear. Here's y'alls bill, you can just go right on up to the register when you're ready and Ethel will ring you up." The waitress handed the bill to Andy and walked two tables down, sounding like a broken record, "So how was everything? Good, that's what we like..."

"Ready?" Andy asked as he started to get up from his chair.

"Yea," Sarah replied as she took one final sip of her water and followed behind him.

Andy went up to the register and paid for both of their lunches. Sarah thanked him and they proceeded back outside to Sarah's car.

The drive back to Sarah's house wasn't a long one, but the silence made it seem to drag on forever. Andy pulled on to the street where Sarah lived and slowed down as he came up to Sarah's house. Andy stopped the car and Sarah unlatched her seatbelt and opened the car door.

"Hold on a second, Sarah," Andy said as he put his right hand on her lap. "I feel like there is something that you aren't telling me. It's like you want to tell me but you can't."

"It's now or never," Sarah thought to herself. "I'm just going through a lot of stuff right now," she again lost her courage to tell him. "You know with losing Dad, and me getting mad at Raymond for not being here, and then the whole thing with Mitch last night, I just have so much going on in my head that I can't think straight."

"What happened between you and Mitch?" Andy asked with a sense of wonder in his tone.

"He came over to the house last night and told me about..." Sarah caught herself. She really didn't want to go into this right now. "Um, he had told me that I shouldn't be so hard on Raymond, that if he said he couldn't make it in then he probably couldn't."

"Oh," Andy replied. "So that's it?"

"Well I was still upset with Raymond so I took my frustration out on Mitch and threw a coffee cup at him."

"Did you hit him?"

"No, it hit the wall beside him and shattered."

"Oh, okay." Andy replied. He was still under the impression that there was something Sarah wasn't telling him. "Well if you need anything I will probably be home all night. So just give me a call or something."

"Thanks. I think I'm just going to clean the house and probably go to bed. I haven't been getting much sleep for the past few days and now that this is all over I think I'll be able to sleep better," Sarah said as she got out of his car and shut the door.

Without looking back at him, Sarah walked up to her front door, unlocked it and then stepped inside. Andy sat there the entire time to see her in, waiting for her to turn around, she never did. Once Sarah shut the door still with her back to him, Andy quickly pulled away from the curb and raced down the street.

Inside, Sarah stood still right inside her house, her back leaning against the front door. Of course Sarah didn't need to clean her house, she always kept it immaculate. Still with her back against the door, Sarah kicked off her black heels, put her keys on the dining room table, and headed into the kitchen. Sarah pulled a glass out of the strainer and filled it with cold water from the faucet. She took a sip from the glass and headed into the bathroom. Sarah stared at her reflection in the mirror of the medicine cabinet. She looked like shit. Tired, bags under her eyes, and her hair was a mess. She opened the medicine cabinet and pulled out a bottle of aspirin. She didn't really have a headache and was hoping that this would help relax her. Sarah cupped her hand and shook the bottle until she was holding two pills. She decided that it wasn't enough and shook the bottle a little more until she held four pills. She put the top back on the bottle and placed it back on the shelf inside her medicine cabinet. Sarah popped the aspirin into her mouth and took a large mouthful of water, swallowing everything in one gulp.

Sarah left her bathroom and began to walk down the hallway and into her room. She thought to herself that she would lay down and rest for a bit. She had felt as if she had been pulled in a million different directions and had been given the weight of the world to carry on her shoulders over the past few days. Still wearing the same dress that she had worn to her father's funeral, Sarah laid down on her bed and shut her eyes.

After what seemed like only seconds, a crack of thunder had startled Sarah. She was shocked to find her room completely dark. Lightening would brighten her room for a couple of seconds and then the darkness would once again fill it.

Sarah fumbled in the dark as she reached across her bed to find the lamp that was sitting on her night stand. She turned it on and rubbed the sleep from her eyes. Looking down at her watch she was shocked to see that it was already twenty past ten.

Sarah didn't feel any better than she had before she went to sleep and she knew what she needed to do. The only thing that would rest her nerves and lift a huge burden was to go and talk to Andy. Sarah changed out of her dress and into a pair of blue jeans with a tan blouse.

139

Sarah walked to her dining room to grab her keys off the table where she had left them hours earlier and left her house. When she turned around to lock her front door, there was a large gust of wind and bright flash. Sarah quickly covered her ears and shut her eyes without thinking, but it was too late. The thunder had already come deafening her momentarily. Once the ringing stopped in her ears, Sarah opened her eyes to a completely dark street. The last lightening strike had taken out the power.

Sarah made a quick dash to her car. By the smell of the air, a down pour was to happen any minute. Once inside her car, Sarah started the engine, pulled away from the curb, and headed south out of town to Andy's house.

Andy lived just past the outskirts of Sumertown in a small house that he had bought when he first moved back to town. The house sat about half a mile off the main highway covered by many trees and invisible from the road.

As Sarah was driving out of town she passed the old Mom & Pop shop where she and Raymond had gone after their mother had committed suicide. Sarah didn't remember anything from that night as she was too young, but the thought was there. She often wondered about how differently her life would have turned out if her parents hadn't got a divorce. Her mother would still be alive, she and Raymond wouldn't have had such a distant relationship with their father, and Raymond may have never met and married Beth.

Just outside of town she came to the road that would lead to Andy's house. Sarah slowed down and pulled onto the gravel road. The full trees covered the lightning show from above. Every few feet that Sarah drove a splatter of rain would make its way through the leaves from above and hit her windshield.

As Sarah rounded a turn she saw Andy's house with just some light coming from the windows. Sarah turned her car lights off and drove around to the back of the house where she stopped and turned the car off.

She felt like her heart was about to pop out of her chest. Adrenalin filled her body as she opened her car door to get out, leaving the keys in the ignition. Slowly, one leg at a time she stepped out of her car and shut her door and proceeded to walk around to the front of Andy's house.

As Sarah rounded the corner to the house she looked in through the front window and saw several lit candles in Andy's living room. He must of also lost power when the town did as Sarah was leaving her home.

Sarah walked in front of the window and paused for just a moment. She thought she had heard someone talking. Frantically, she looked all around her staring off into the dark forest hoping that no one was out there with her. Once she had satisfied both her nerves and mind she headed for the front door.

Sarah reached down for the doorknob and found it unlocked. As she opened the door she again thought she heard voices, only this time it was coming from inside the house. It almost sounded as if someone was laughing. Sarah's heart was now racing.

"Andy?" She called out. But only a whisper came through her lips. Again she called out and as before a faint whisper was all she could produce. She could feel her heart pounding as she began to wonder what was really going on inside Andy's house.

Sarah just stood there, unable to move. She kept trying to get herself to move forward, but her legs kept her concreted in place. Just as she was able to take her first step she heard the voices again, only this time it was much clearer.

"Andy, stop it. Oh you've been so bad."

"Well you know what you should do with a bad boy, don't you?"

There was no denying who those voices belonged to, Andy and Beth. With the laughter and moaning coming from one of the rooms there wasn't much left to the imagination to know what was going on.

Sarah was devastated. For the first time she knew for a fact that this affair was a reality and not just something the gossip mill had turned out. Anger and sadness filled her body as Sarah turned around and walked out of Andy's house. Slowly Sarah began to walk back around the house to where she had parked her car.

Sarah got in her car and shut the door. For a moment Sarah simply stared out the windshield in a daze. So many thoughts were running through her mind and she couldn't concentrate on just one to make any sense out of what had just happened. Then she lost it.

"WHY?" Sarah screamed out hysterically as she sobbed. "WHY, WHY, WHY?" She asked repeatedly while hitting the steering wheel with both of her hands. Sarah rested her forehead on the steering wheel and shook it back and forth as she continued to cry.

She need a tissue to wipe her eyes and grabbed her purse that was sitting in the passenger seat. She set it on her lap and unzipped the top. Wiping away the tears from her eyes with her hand she reached in to grab a tissue. However, the first thing that her fingers grasped was a hard piece of steel.

Sarah looked down and pulled the gun from her purse, gazing at it. She held the gun in her right hand and twisted her wrist back and forth, up and down looking at all angles of the gun. A flash of lightening coming from above seemed to jolt her back into reality. All of a sudden the tears stopped and a sense of peace came over Sarah. She held the gun in front of her face looking at it very carefully and then slowly turned her head towards Andy's house and opened her car door.

* * * * * * * * *

"Wait a minute," Bobby said as he looked up from the notes that he had been writing. "I want to make sure I have this right. Was this the same night that Andy was murdered?"

"Yes," Sarah nodded, "yes, it was." There were several puzzled looks in the room.

"Grandma Sara, I've read nearly every article you have here on your brother's trial and there was never any mention of you being at Andy's house the night that he was murdered. In fact, the papers mention very little about you at all."

"I know," Sarah replied.

"And you're sure that this was the same night, Mom?" Kyle asked.

"I'm positive," she answered as she turned her head to meet her son's eyes.

"But it's like Bobby said, all of these articles never..."

"Don't you get it?" Sarah asked cutting Kyle off. "The papers, the courts, the lawyers they all belong to their own little group. Their number one priority back then was to watch out for each other. You have no idea how many things have been covered up by these people. They tell and portray events as they want you to believe it." Sarah's listeners looked on in shock. "Everything," she said pointing to the clippings still on her bed, "everything in those papers are lies. The only bit of truth is that they found my Raymond guilty. Guilty of a murder he never committed. Now, I'm going to tell you all what really happened on the night the lights went out in Georgia."

* * * * * * * * *

Slowly Sarah began to get out of the car, the entire time her eyes remained fixed on the house. Once she had exited her vehicle she gently pushed the door closed as to not cause a loud slamming noise.

For a moment, she just stood there. She was bent over with her arms rested on the hood of the car with the gun in her right hand.

There was now a slight breeze and off in the distance Sarah heard the rumble of thunder. There was another storm approaching. As she leaned there, she asked herself two questions: How was she going to do it? Who was going to be the first one to go?

To begin with, Sarah thought about shooting Beth first. That way Andy could see what kind of mess he had caused and gotten himself into. But then she thought about killing Andy first. That way she could tell Beth exactly what she thought of her and how much of a fucking slut she thought she was. Then the icing on the cake was going to be raising the gun and watching Beth beg and plead for her life before she pulled the trigger. A smile came across Sarah's face thinking of that. She could just see Beth screaming, sobbing, and pleading. Beth and Andy both deserved what they had coming.

Back and forth these thoughts occupied Sarah's mind until she finally decided that the first step she needed to take was that of the one in the direction of the house. Only once she was inside would she actually decide who the lucky one was going to be.

Pushing herself back from the car she began to walk towards the front of the house. As she made her way to the door she could again hear their voices coming from inside. This time instead of welling up, hatred filled her body. Sarah decided to tuck the gun in the back of her pants. This would be yet another element of her surprise.

Sarah was now standing at Andy's front door. She reached for the doorknob and gave it a turn. This time she found it was locked. Maybe they had heard her when she left minutes earlier and they got spooked. With her left hand she reached into her pocket for her keys. "What kind of idiot gives his girlfriend a key to his place and then cheats on her in the same damn house?" Sarah muttered under her breath as she found the right key and inserted it into the lock.

The door unlocked easily with just a small click. Sarah froze for just a moment, from the sound of things inside they couldn't have heard the lock. Sarah pulled the key out and put it back in her pocket. Again she grabbed the doorknob and began to slowly turn it. Once she had it turned as far as it would go she extended her arm to open the door.

Sarah could now hear the two of them very clearly. Once the door was completely opened she stepped into the house. She was standing in Andy's living room. She noticed lit candles were scattered throughout the room. The back of the couch was facing her and she knew it was blocking her view of them.

Slowly, Sarah began to proceed further in the living room. With each step that she took, she could see more of what was in front of the couch. It started with the corner of a blanket, then a leg and in just a couple more steps, there on the floor, were Andy and Beth.

He was on his side with his back to her with his shirt off. Sarah could only make out Beth's arm around Andy's neck. They laid there together on the floor making out. A blanket was covering the bottom half of them.

For a few seconds Sarah stood there watching. Although she had been told about the affair it seemed to really impact her more at this moment as she was witnessing it with her very own eyes a mere couple of feet in front of her.

"So, is she a good fuck?" Sarah asked as she leaned forward on the couch with the palm of her hands resting on the top of it.

"Sarah!" Beth yelled as she jumped to her feet wearing a piece of sky blue lingerie. She quickly reached down and yanked the blanket off of Andy to cover herself.

"Oh my God Sarah, what are you doing here?" Andy asked as he began to slowly make his way to his feet wearing only a pair of boxers.

"What am I doing here?" Sarah asked out loud in a sarcastic tone throwing her hand up in the air. "What am I doing here? What the hell is she doing here?" Sarah yelled as she angrily pointed her finger at Beth.

"Look Sarah, just calm down and let's talk about this," Andy said quietly with an almost comforting tone in his voice.

"Calm down?" Sarah snapped back. "How in the hell do you expect me to calm down? You're cheating on me with my brother's wife." They both stared into each other's eyes for a few seconds. There, standing in front of her, was the man that she had fallen in love with. Sarah's emotions began to take over as her eyes filled with tears. "Dammit Andy, I loved you. I gave you my heart and soul, my entire life. Jesus I wanted to have children with you and I find out this is what you are doing behind my back!" Sarah tried to rub the tears away from her eyes.

"Sarah, I'm so sorry. You have to believe me that I never wanted to hurt you. And regardless of what you may think, I do still love you," Andy said.

Beth simply snorted at that and Sarah glared at her. Beth quickly looked away and clutched the blanket even closer to body.

"Why did you do it? Was I really that bad that you had to go out and get satisfaction from someone else?"

"No, you weren't. Honestly I just don't think I was ready to be settled down with just one girl," Andy answered.

There was only silence now. Andy couldn't think of anything more to say to try and make things better, Beth didn't dare utter a word and Sarah had so much to say but was having difficulties turning her thoughts into words.

"You know you have just thrown our entire relationship away don't you? We're over," Sarah told Andy.

"Sarah, we can work this out. You are still the one I want to be with," Andy said.

"Excuse me?" Beth blurted out. "And where does that leave me?"

Just the sound of Beth's voice was enough to bring Sarah's blood pressure up. She could feel her face getting warm.

"Beth, please," Andy said.

"No Andy, we have something. I felt it and I know you felt it over and over again," Beth said.

"I can't believe this," Sarah said throwing her hands up into the air as she backed away from the couch. "You're a pig," she said looking at Andy. "And you're nothing more than a whore," Sarah said to Beth. She turned around and started walking towards the front door.

"Well you can call me whatever you want, however, if you knew how to keep Andy happy he wouldn't have had to come running to me, begging for it time and time again," responded Beth.

Sarah stopped dead in her tracks. She clenched her hands into fists and turned around to see Beth standing there with her hand on her hip, her head slightly cocked and the blanket no longer covering her. That bitch.

"You know Beth, I'm a firm believer in what goes around comes around," Sarah said as she slowly reached behind her back. "And even though this may not completely fit into the category..." in one swift motion Sarah pulled the gun from the back of her pants, quickly raised it up pointing it at Beth and cocked the gun, "the end result is still the same. You're fucked."

Before Beth even had a chance to react with a scream or to even get out of the way, Sarah closed her left eye, lined up the shot and fired the gun. Beth was dead before her body even hit the floor with a single gunshot wound to the head.

"Jesus Christ, what the hell is wrong with you?" Andy cried out as he started to make his way over to Beth.

"Don't move," Sarah said as she cocked the gun and pointed it at him. Andy did as she said. "Now, can you give me one good reason why you shouldn't be joining her on the floor?"

"Sarah," Andy said in a panic, his forehead covered in sweat. "You had no right, I mean you, she's, I can't believe you killed her."

"That one was for Raymond."

"Raymond? Are you nuts? He already knew about all of this," Andy said.

"No, he knew that she was having an affair, he just didn't know that it was with you."

"Yes he did, well kind of. I talked to Raymond earlier."

"What are you talking about? Raymond's in Candletop."

"No, he's home. We talked at Web's tonight. He told me that he thought Beth was cheating on him and wanted to know if I knew anything about it. I told him that I knew she had been sleeping with Seth and rumor had it she was also seeing the judge on the side. He got pretty upset and that's when I just blurted out that I had also been with her a couple of times," Andy explained.

"You're a liar," Sarah said. "Why would you tell him that you were sleeping with Beth?"

"I told him that I had, not that I currently was. I felt guilty, I mean he's my best friend. Yea I had had a few drinks and wasn't thinking too clearly when I told him, but at the time it just seemed like the right thing to do. Besides, part of me also thought that if he went home and approached Beth about it then she was going to tell him about us." Andy once again looked over at Beth's lifeless body laying on the floor, a pool of blood growing larger from beneath her head.

"And what did he say?"

"Nothing. He gave me the worst look that made me absolutely sick to my stomach. He got up from the table and stormed out of the place."

"So you thought it would help make things better to have Beth over here for one of your secret hook ups?"

"No, I had her over to break things off and then one thing led to another and that's when you showed up."

"And what reason do I have to believe you?"

"None Sarah. You have absolutely no reason in the world to believe me. But you have to listen to me. Everything is going to be okay. We can get through this whole situation together. I'll be by your side every step of the way. But first, I just need for you to give me the gun."

Andy held his hand out for the gun. Sarah still had it pointed at him. Her eyes moved quickly back and forth between Beth's body and Andy's eyes.

"No," she said.

"Sarah, seriously. You need to give me the gun."

"I said no!"

"Sarah, don't be so damn stupid. Now, give me the gun before anyone else gets hurt." Andy's tone was demanding.

Sarah shook her head no but couldn't say anything. She didn't feel the hatred that she had just a few minutes ago, or the betrayal when she first got to Andy's house. Instead she now felt afraid. What had she done? What was going to happen to her? If she gave Andy the gun would he try to shoot her?

"SARAH!" Andy yelled. Sarah stood there, her arm still stretched out. The gun now felt very heavy in her hand and she found it difficult it to keep her arm steady. "Fine, I'll get it myself." Andy stepped onto the couch that was separating them and then fell backwards onto the floor landing on his back.

* * * * * * * * *

Looking up from a newspaper that she had been holding, Sarah looked around the room at each of her guests taking in the way each of them looked after hearing the story that she had held inside of her for so long.

Bobby sat there with his mouth hanging open and his pencil laying flat on his pad of paper. Josh showed very little emotion. In fact, the look on his face seemed to say that he already knew what Sarah had done, and maybe he did. He was, after all, a brilliant man and perhaps when Sarah had started in on her story he was able to connect the dots early on and had already jumped ahead to the ending. Brooke sat in her chair with her arms folded in her lap and her eyes glassed over with tears. Then finally there was her son, Kyle. His elbows had been resting on his knees with his hands cradling his head. As he looked up, Sarah could see that his face was pale. He looked at his mother with disgust. Here was the woman that for his entire life he had placed on a pedestal, and now he found out that she was a cold blooded murderer.

Sarah cleared her throat before continuing on with her story. "The second time I honestly didn't remember pulling the trigger. I think out of reaction when Andy started coming towards me I had just reacted. I honestly hadn't had any time to aim and initially when he had fallen backwards I thought it was because he had lost his balance. It wasn't until I approached the couch and looked down at him that I saw his chest covered in blood. Later the, coroner's report would state that the bullet had hit a major artery. He never felt a thing, neither one of us did."

"And does that upset you? Are you mad because they didn't feel any pain cause that was all part of your plan? Let them lay there in pain and agony as life slowly left their body? I mean that is what you wanted, wasn't it?" Kyle scolded as he picked his head up out of his hands and met his mother's eyes.

"Kyle," Brooke said as she put her hand on his lap.

"No, I can't be here," Kyle said as he got up from his chair.

"Sweetie, please understand, that was a long, long time ago," Sarah said looking up at her son.

"Mom, what you did was wrong. It was wrong in so many ways. What gives you the right to take another person's life, two people for that matter?" Without giving his mother the chance to respond, Kyle walked out of her ICU room, down the hall, and out of sight from Sarah.

"I'll go get him," Brooke said.

"No, let him be," Sarah replied. "He's probably thinking that I've lied to him his entire life. Just give him some time to himself and he'll be okay."

"Okay Sarah," Josh said. It had been the first time he had said anything to her in awhile. "You do realize what you've just gotten yourself into? This is pre-meditated murder, murder one. They will definitely get you for murder one on Beth. We could always claim self defense and get murder two on Andy. But after the doctors clear you and after your trial, you will spend the rest of your life behind bars."

"It doesn't matter, Josh," Sarah said in her old frail voice. "I'm an old woman and right now, time is not on my side. I knew and understood what would happen to me when I told you this story. I only have one favor to ask of you." Josh simply nodded his head. "Don't say anything yet. Please let me finish this story so I can put my soul to rest. I've already come this far and I have to get the rest of it out." Again, Josh simply nodded his head.

"Grandma Sarah, I'm confused about a couple of things. You say that you killed this Beth. But after reading a couple of these articles they have all come to the same conclusion, Beth skipped town after Raymond found out about her cheating on him," Bobby stated.

"You see, it all goes back to what I said earlier. They report what they want you to know. The truth is, nobody knew where she was, not even my Raymond," Sarah answered.

"Okay, then how do you explain how it was that your brother was found guilty of a crime that he never committed?" Bobby questioned.

"I'm getting there," Sarah said. "I knew that I needed to get rid of the bodies before anyone found out what I had done. I figured I'd start with Beth since she was the smallest of the two.

"To avoid making a bigger mess I took the blanket that she had covered herself with earlier and wrapped it around her head. The last thing I wanted was a trail of blood throughout the house. After wrapping her head, I grabbed both of her ankles and began to slowly walk backwards. I was surprised at how heavy her body was and that got me to thinking exactly where the expression dead weight came from.

"Once through the living room I had made it into the kitchen which was at the back of the house. I dropped Beth's ankles, unlocked the back door and opened it. A nice warm breeze was blowing and the smell of rain still filled the night air. I bent back down and picked up Beth's ankles, kicked the screen door open with my left foot, and proceeded outside. It was kind of awkward pulling her body through the doorway all while trying to keep the screen door from closing and hitting me or getting hung up on her body. Once we had cleared the threshold, I proceeded down the three wooden steps. Each step that I took was followed by a thud as Beth's skull came cracking down on the steps.

"I found that it was much more difficult to pull Beth through the yard. I kept slipping on the wet marshy grass, but knew that I had to make it to right past my car where the forest began. There, mixed among the trees, was an old well that was used back before the house that Andy was living in had indoor plumbing. I knew that it would be the perfect spot to hide both bodies as not many people knew that it existed. I knew about the well because Andy and I had found it one night when we were out walking in the woods. We thought it would be fun to walk through the woods after a few drinks and see how scared we could make ourselves. I was all game for it at the time. After going only a short distance my flashlight had caught the stones that circled the well. It no longer had the overhang where you could drop a bucket and pull it back up full of water. The only thing that remained were the stones. In fact, nothing even covered the top. So naturally, at the time, it seemed like the perfect spot to dispose the two of them.

"I figured once I got both bodies in there I would began to fill the well with dirt, forever incasing their bodies in this tomb. Finally, after dragging Beth what seemed like the length of a football field, I was at the well. The next thing for me to determine at that time was how I was going to drop the body without it getting lodged at some point in between before it reached the bottom. I had estimated that the opening to the well was somewhere around four feet. As long as I dropped the body straight down there would be no problem. However, if while the body fell, it would hunch over, there would be a major problem.

"I really don't know what made me decide to drop her body head first but that is what I did. I had ahold of her ankles and made a half circle until her head was now facing the well.

"I propped her up against the well and again began to try to pick her up from underneath her arms. Halfway up, I thought I heard the crunching of gravel. That must have jump started my muscles because I remember my heart began to pound even harder and before I knew it, I had Beth's body sitting on top of the well.

"I paused for only a moment to stop and listen, but I didn't hear any other noises. I figured it must have been the wind or the approaching storm. Since I had assured myself that there was no one else out there with me, I began to slowly lay Beth down. Her body was now half hunched over the opening. I grabbed her by the ankles and began to slowly walk her body into the well letting gravity pull her towards the bottom. The further I pushed, the heavier her body became. Finally I was at the end, her body was parallel with the shaft and with my hands still grasped firmly on her ankles, I let go. After just a split second I heard a snap and then a splash. I was relieved when I heard the splash because I knew that she had made it all the way to the bottom. However, my mind was set on that snap that I heard. It must of been the sound of her neck snapping as it hit the side of the well during her final decent to her grave.

"For the first time, I became so sick to my stomach that I actually threw up. I honestly don't know why, but there was just something about that noise that I couldn't stand.

"Once I had regained composure over myself, I started to head back to the house. From out of nowhere the wind began to blow violently. I reached the screen door to the back of the house and as I opened it, the wind ripped it right out of my hand. With a loud bang and rattle it hit the side of the house. I grabbed the handle again and pulled the door shut as I stepped back inside Andy's house."

* * * * * * * * *

Sarah stood there for just a moment listening to the howling of the wind behind her. She was standing in the kitchen looking down the short hall that led to the living room where she knew Andy's body was lying.

As Sarah began to walk down the hall, her nerves began to get the better of her. She began thinking to herself that when she entered the living room she would see Andy standing there, in a pool of his own blood, asking her why.

She cautiously proceeded into the living room, slowly leaning forward so she could peak into the room. Andy's body was still there, in the same position she had left it just a few minutes earlier. She knew now that she had to get his body into the well.

A loud clap of thunder shook the house. Sarah's heart jumped as she thought she saw someone else in the room. She stood there moving only her eyes. The front door was open but all she could see was darkness. The wind must have blown out the candles. There was a flash of lightning that briefly illuminated the outside, and there, standing in the doorway, was the silhouette of a person.

Motionless Sarah stood there, holding her breath thinking that if this person couldn't see her, they would definitely be able to hear her breathing. Now only darkness. She waited for the next bolt of lightning to flash to see if there was actually a person there or if her mind was merely playing tricks on her.

Flash.

This time the doorway stood empty but the window showed someone peering in. Darkness. Sarah hunched down behind the couch hoping that the intruder hadn't seen her.

Flash.

Back at the screen door.

Now she could hear the squeaking of the wooden floor. What the hell was she going to do now? There was no way out for her. Who was this? What were they going to do with her?

Flash.

The shadow of the person now reflected across the living room and cast its shadow on the wall.

All of a sudden there was a light. This person had turned on a flashlight. She could hear them walking, each step getting closer to her. Sarah's heart was racing, her body began to quiver uncontrollably in fear. She began to find it hard to catch her breath. Sarah could see the beam from the flashlight sweeping back and forth in the living room with each step that they took.

Then the light stopped moving and was now fixed on Andy's lifeless body. Sarah could see the light shake, shake as if this person was just as petrified as she was.

"What the hell?"

Sarah turned all her attention to that faint whisper she heard. A feeling of reassurance took over. She knew exactly who that voice belonged to and knew that they had to be there for a reason.

"Raymond?" Sarah whispered out.

Immediately the room was filled with the sound of a yell and the loud thud of the flashlight hitting the floor.

"Who's in here?" Raymond called out with panic filling his voice as the beam of the flashlight was now going around in circles.

"Raymond, it's Sarah." She stood up from in front of the couch just as Raymond turned towards where he heard the voice come from. The flashlight was now focused on her face and Sarah squinted at the bright light. "Raymond, I've done something bad."

"Sarah. Jesus Christ what happened?" Raymond had now lowered the flashlight from his sister's face and once again found it shining on Andy's lifeless body.

"I don't really know. All I wanted to do was scare him, but I thought he was coming after me and then he was on the, and then he...I didn't hear the gun fire." Sarah again found herself getting worked up and fighting to catch her breath.

"Just calm down. Did anyone know that you were coming out here?"

"No," Sarah replied.

"Did anyone see you drive out here?"

"I don't think so."

"Okay, we can handle this. First, we need to call the, no wait that's not right. We need to get rid of the body. Yes...that's the best thing right now."

"I know, that's just what I was trying to do. I remember there being an old well back behind the house. I was just out there and got the cover taken off of it." Sarah obviously lied because she couldn't bring herself to tell Raymond that she had just put his wife in that same well.

"Sarah, you need to get out of here. You have got too much going for you to end up with blood on your hands. Just get on home and I'll take care of this. But why did you come over here in the first place?"

Sarah couldn't bear to tell Raymond that Beth had been unfaithful to him. She figured it would just be best to tell him only part of the truth.

"Raymond, he cheated on me," Sarah told him. "Sure, part of me really did want to kill him when I found out and I had actually practiced shooting one of Dad's guns. But it was in my purse and I forgot about it and then," Sarah paused. She didn't want to tell him that Beth was actually here and what had just happened, she needed to come up with a believable lie, something that wouldn't sound too fake and that she could convince him had actually happened. "When I got here, I asked him about it and before I knew it, we were yelling at each other and he wouldn't be completely honest with me. So I stormed back out to my car and got the gun. I was only going to flash it at him to show him I meant business. But then, I just don't know how it all happened."

"Ok. I'll get rid of the body, clean up this mess and this will just be something that will forever stay between the two of us," Raymond told her as he walked around the couch to give Sarah a hug.

"Thank you so much, Raymond," Sarah said melting into his arms. "I don't know what I would do without you."

"I'm here for you. I know I wasn't earlier today, but I am here for you now."

Sarah had almost forgotten about her father's funeral from just a few hours earlier. After all that had happened, it seemed like she had buried her father years ago.

"It doesn't matter Raymond, all that matters is that you are here now."

"Ok, let's go. You show me where this well is and then get your ass out of here."

Sarah thought for a second. Would it be possible for Raymond to see Beth's body resting at the bottom of the well? No, surely not. Wells are deep and it was dark out. No, he wouldn't see anything...or would he?

"Come on Sarah, we got to get moving. Why is there so much blood in here?"

Sarah wondered if Raymond would be able to guess that all the blood on the floor had actually come from two bodies. She simply didn't answer her brother and began to walk back toward the end of the house, when all of a sudden the living room was illuminated in a bright red light, then a blue light, and back to red. Both Sarah and Raymond turned around and gazed towards the front door, the room still flashing with lights back and forth between red and blue. Police.

"Raymond, it's the police. But how could they..."

"Get out of here, Sarah. Just run," Raymond whispered to her as he gently pushed her aside.

"No Raymond, this is my fault," Sarah began to plead to her brother.

"I'll take care of this, just go."

"But Raymond..."

"GET OUT OF HERE!"

Those words triggered a reaction like a marathon runner taking off at a gun shot. Sarah immediately ran back into the kitchen through the backdoor, past her car, past the well and began to run deep into the forest behind Andy's house.

She had no idea where she was running to nor did she know what was ahead of her. All she knew was that she didn't want to get caught. Her hands reached in front of her pushing aside branches and limbs. It didn't do much as she kept feeling them hit her in the face.

Something caught Sarah on the leg and she went tumbling face first into the soggy ground. Sarah stood back up trying to catch her breath. She strained to see if there was anything she could hear coming from the direction she had just ran from. But there was nothing. No police, no guns, nobody yelling, only silence. She wondered what was going on back at Andy's house. Surely by now the police would have seen Andy's lifeless body lying there. But what about Raymond? Why hadn't he ran out with her?

Sarah kept thinking to herself that this had to be some kind of a nightmare. She was going to wake up any minute now and she would be in her bed, in her room, in her house. None of this would have ever happened. She would break things off with Andy, tell Raymond about Beth and then everyone would go on about their new lives.

But standing in the dark woods, Sarah knew that this wasn't going to end by just waking up. She looked off into the distance towards the house but couldn't see anything. How long had it been? She didn't know what to think. By this point she had caught her breath, but the pressure in her chest was still there. The fear of not knowing what was going on, what would happen to her once she got back to the house, of what was going to happen to Raymond after the police came into Andy's house.

Sarah had lost track of time and didn't know exactly how long she had been standing in the woods. At a much slower pace Sarah began to back track her steps and make her way to Andy's house. What was the punishment for murder? She knew that Raymond could get the chair. Other states they would surely have hung him. But not here. Everyone knew what a great guy Raymond was. And everyone in town knew about Andy and Beth. They would take it easy on him. Everyone in town would come to his defense. Yea he would probably go to jail for a few years but that would be it.

Over and over again Sarah kept reassuring herself that everything was going to be okay. Raymond had always been there for her and this wasn't going to change anything. He'd do his time and then be right back to watching over his little sister.

Sarah could now start to make out the house through the trees. As she began to make her way slowly past the well she almost expected to see Beth's hand reach up and pull her body up out of there. The very thought sent shivers down her spine. Just past the woods she was now standing in the back yard. Her car was still parked there. She couldn't see any lights flashing from either side of the house so she assumed the cops were already gone.

She wanted to go into the house and see if Andy's body was still there, or if they had already removed it. But she decided not to. Sarah walked over to her car, got inside and started the engine. She put the car in reverse and began to back out to the highway and then headed home.

* * * * * * * * *

"I didn't sleep at all that night," Sarah continued from her hospital bed. "As soon as I got home I immediately got in the shower, somehow convincing myself that the hot water would wash away the guilt I was feeling. Not for the murders, because till this day I still won't apologize for what happened that night, but the guilt for Raymond. While I was standing there in my shower I had no idea what was happening to my brother. I only assumed that by now he was probably in the middle of being questioned. Or that he was sitting on some hard bed in a dark nasty cell.

"I had decided that I would refuse to let him take the rap. I was going to confess to the murders. For once in my life I wasn't going to allow Raymond to bail me out of a mess."

Silence was circled around Sarah. Here was a woman that everyone thought the world of, considered her to be a saint, and in the span of only a few hours, had just confessed to a double homicide.

By now Bobby had stopped writing and was looking at the woman he called "Grandma Sarah" all his life in utter disbelief. She always had lemonade for him in the summer when he would stop by as a child. Sarah was even the one that helped Bobby get the job at the paper after seeing what kind of work he did for the local high school paper. Now he was supposed to reveal to everyone in town the skeletons in Sarah's closet.

Josh had uncrossed his legs and was now shaking his head. He had tried so many different murders in the past where he would try to avoid the death penalty or life in prison for his clients. And he was good at it. But after each trial when he knew for a fact that his client was as guilty as the day is long he often wished worse would have happened. An eye for an eye was what he believed in. That's why he tried to stay away from murder trials. Never did he think he would have to defend one of his dearest friends in one. And yet, his mentality of thinking had changed and honestly saw Sarah as the victim in this situation.

Brooke, sitting next to Sarah, had tears coming from her eyes, yet she didn't make a sound. She looked at Sarah as an incredible woman that held this horrible tragedy inside her for all these years. She was so proud of her and yet was very afraid of what would come.

"Sarah, I don't even know where to begin with all of this. You do realize that once I get home I'm going to have to talk to the police and tell them what you've done? I'm really sorry, but it has to be done," Josh said empathetically.

"Josh, don't you get it? I'm nearly at peace with all of this. Whatever happens will happen. I'm not worried and neither should you. But," Sarah started up again looking at her audience, "I really did try to tell them that he was innocent, that they had made a horrible mistake. But, they all thought I was crazy."

7

IT'S ALL OVER

In the morning, Sarah got herself dressed and decided that first thing she needed to do was go down to the police station to make things right. As she walked out her house she put her sunglasses on and headed to her car. The sun was bright and the humidity heavy. All around her she saw her neighbors all stop what they were doing and look over in her direction. There was no doubt that the news had already spread throughout town and that everybody had heard that Raymond had shot and killed Andy.

"I hate this damn town," Sarah muttered to herself as she got to her car and put her key into the door to unlock it.

"Sarah?" asked a voice from the sidewalk. Sarah turned around and saw Sheila Holsworth walking up the drive to her. "Sarah, are you ok?"

Sheila was one of those busy bodies in town. She would be your best friend over coffee and gossip and then as soon as she was out of your sight would go and tell one of her other friends that she just couldn't believe how you kept your house and would over-exaggerate everything.

"Excuse me?" Sarah said as she turned to face her. She was in no mood for any of Sheila's crap.

"We've been so worried about you and with everything about Raymond."

"What are you talking about, Sheila?"

"You haven't heard," Sheila gasped. She stood there looking at Sarah searching for an answer in her body language. "Oh my goodness, you haven't?"

"Look, don't believe everything you hear on the streets."

"But Sarah, sweetie, it's in the papers. We've been coming to check on you for the last couple of days, but you never answered your door."

Sarah was confused. What did Sheila mean that it had been in the papers? The paper in Sumertown wasn't delivered until the evening. And why would they have been checking on her? Sheila actually stood before her and had a look of concern.

Looking around she saw the neighbors were all still looking at her, some had migrated together and were in small groups. Looking around her yard Sarah saw several rolled up newspapers. What was going on?

"Sheila," Sarah said as she took her sunglasses off. "What exactly was said about Raymond in the paper?"

"Oh sugar, I'm sorry to have to be the one to break this to you. But Andy's gone. Raymond killed him," Sheila began to well up.

"I know that," Sarah said frustrated. "But how in the hell is it in the paper? That just happened last night."

"No. No, it happened a few days ago."

"No Sheila, it happened yesterday. Yesterday I'm telling you. I buried my father yesterday. Raymond came home from Candletop yesterday."

"Sarah, today's June 3rd. Are you ok?"

In that very instant Sarah began to feel light headed. How could so many days have passed and she not realize it. No this was all wrong. The whole town was against her and setting her up. "You're a liar." Sarah said as she opened her car door.

"Sarah I'm telling you the truth. That all happened a few days ago. We wondered why you never showed up for the trial. We understood why for the hanging, but not for the trial."

"WHAT?" Sarah yelled as she spun around and grabbed both of Sheila's shoulders hard. "WHAT THE HELL DID YOU JUST SAY?"

By now Sheila was very frightened. "Aaaabout the trial?"

"No after that," Sarah's throat was dry, the lump was moving up her throat.

"The hangin'?"

"What hanging Sheila?" Sarah was now in tears "WHAT HANGING?"

"Raymond's," she whispered. "They found him guilty and hung him two days ago."

The words 'hung him' seemed to echo in Sarah's head. She couldn't believe what she was hearing. A numbness took over her body and she felt as though her legs were about to give out from beneath her. She leaned up against her car for support. Slowly she began to see the neighbors cross the street and walk towards her house.

One by one they each came up and were saying something to her. She couldn't hear them and they began to blur as the tears flooded her eyes. She tried to remain as calm and composed as possible. There was no way, it was impossible, nearly three days that she couldn't recall.

Sarah looked down at her feet and then out of the corner of her eye she saw several newspapers scattered in the lawn. She quickly pushed the few people that had gathered in her drive way out of the way and rushed over. She bent down and pulled the first one out of the protective plastic wrap, took the rubber band off, and unrolled it. May 29 & 30. It was the Friday Saturday weekend edition. She turned around and saw two more papers laying side by side. She scooped down and picked up another one. Again, as before, she ripped it open and looked at the date. It was Tuesday, June 2, 1953. The very first headline read, 'Turner Pleads Guilty & Immediately Hung."

Sarah fell to the ground weeping. "He didn't do it," she kept repeating over and over. A few people came to her side and slowly helped her up. "He didn't do it, I did." She told each of them. They all shook their heads as if they agreed but all thought she had gone crazy.

"Come on sugar, let's get you inside," Sheila said as she began to lead Sarah by the arm.

"I can't, I need to go to the police station."

"What for honey?"

"I told you," Sarah said wiping tears off of her cheek. "Raymond was innocent, it was me, I'm the murderer."

"Sugar, you're just grieving and it's okay. Now come on, let's go," Sheila said as she pulled on Sarah's arm.

"Didn't you hear me? Did any of you just hear a single word I said? I DID IT!" Sarah was now screaming. Nobody was paying her any attention and could have cared less that her loving brother had been killed for something she had done.

A few of the neighbors backed a little away and Sheila let go of Sarah's arm. For a moment they all just stood there and looked at the mess Sarah had become. They had no idea what to make of it.

"He told me to run. He told me to get out of there and I did. And now he's gone and it's all my fault." Sarah began to walk towards her front door still weeping and shaking her head. She turned around and still saw everyone standing there. This infuriated her. "Get out of here," she said. Mirroring the same words her brother had said to her just days earlier. "All of you GET OUT OF HERE!" Sarah stormed back inside her house and slammed the door shut.

Inside she leaned her back against the door and sobbed. What was she going to do now? She felt like there was nobody in town she could trust any more, the closest person in her life was now dead.

As she began to walk through her house she noticed it was a disaster. There were broken dishes in the kitchen, items in the living room had been turned over and there was waded up paper littering the floor. It looked like she had been robbed. How in the hell had she missed this just minutes before when she left the house?

She needed to get the whole house cleaned but what intrigued her was all the paper that was lying around. She picked up a few of the balls of paper and sat on the couch. She took the first one and unwrinkled it to read what it said. It was a note to Raymond. In it she kept apologizing over and over and telling him what a wonderful brother he was and how blessed she was to have him in her life.

The second one she opened was a confession letter to the police going into graphic details of not only both murders but also how the two of them had both deserved to die. This was more than a confession letter, it was a hate letter.

Sarah began to open more of them to see what they read. A lot of them had only one or two lines written and she had messed it up waded it up and started again. Others were to some friends telling them that she was sorry for what she had done and how she would be going to jail.

She again reached for another piece of crumpled up paper. She opened it up and began to read it. This one really took her by surprise.

"To those I've left behind. There have been so many things that have gone terribly wrong today. And right now the guilt in my gut is unbearable so I'm dealing with it in the only way I know how.

First you have to know that my brother Raymond is innocent. He didn't kill anybody. He simply did what he has

170

done for me for my entire life, protect me. But this time I cannot and will not allow it.

You have the wrong person. It was me that killed Andy. I really didn't mean to do it, everything just happened so fast. So please, I'm begging you, let my brother go. The only thing he is guilty of is being the perfect brother.

Also to put aside any rumors that may be out there. Yes, Beth and Andy were having an affair. It infuriates me thinking about her and the hurt that she has caused to my Raymond. Well I can tell you this, she won't be hurting anybody anymore. You see, I found out that I don't ever miss when I aim my gun.

Raymond, I know she is your wife and from the bottom of my heart I am truly sorry that I have taken away from you one of the most important people in your life. I would understand if you never forgave me and after this, did away with any memory of me. But always know that my love for you was greater than anything you could have imagined. You were more than a brother to me, you were my parents, and my best friend.

That is why I have decided to take care of this in my own way. By the time you find me it will be too late. I don't know how many or what kind of mixture of medication I just consumed. I simply emptied all the bottles in my medicine cabinet and took them all and will be finishing off this bottle of Merlot. I only hope that once I'm finished with this letter I will go to sleep and never wake up.

Lastly, to everyone in town that knew what was going on, all I have to say is shame on you. You let my brother and I go around looking stupid being in love with these two people when you knew they were screwing around behind our backs. I hope that this letter and the guilt will continue to haunt your dreams for the rest of your pathetic miserable lives.

171

Sincerely---Sarah"

* * * * * * * * *

"It all made perfect sense," Sarah said as she laid down the crumpled piece of paper she had just read from. "I didn't kill myself, obviously but must have either put myself into such a deep tranz that I had no idea what was going on around me for those few days.

"By now I was torn as to what I needed to do. If I went to the police station to tell them what I had done, they would probably look at me as the sister who had gone crazy. If the neighbors didn't believe me why would the police. The only thing that would get them to take me seriously is if I told them about Beth. I knew that I wouldn't be able to keep going through life with this horrible weight constantly following me around."

"Something doesn't make sense," Bobby said as he looked around the room wondering if anyone else was thinking what he was. "Why did your brother go over to Andy's house the night that he got back into town? And how did the police know to show up there?"

That sent off a chain reaction of confused looks with the other two people in the room. It was a very valid point. Raymond had been on the road for a couple of weeks because of his job and when he gets home he goes to see his friend.

"Bobby, you are such a smart young man. You know you're going to go far in this business don't you? You know exactly how to fill in the gaps and ask the right questions.

"Remember what I told you Andy had said to me? He actually told me that he had told Raymond that he and Beth had been sleeping together," Sarah said with her frail voice. "It wasn't until I received a phone call from the police station on that same day that I realized everything that had happened.

"Naturally my heart jumped into my throat when the cop introduced himself over the phone and asked if I knew where Beth could be found. Of course I lied and said that I didn't and asked what it was concerning. There was the matter of picking up the personal belongings that Raymond had had on him on the night that he was arrested.

"After I hung up the phone I got into my car and drove over to the police station. The entire way over I was an emotional wreck. I was still trying to deal with the shock of my brother being hung for my own crime.

"I walked into the police station and several of the officers came up to me to offer their condolences. My voice and body shook violently out of fear. Deep down I thought that they knew I was the guilty one and that they were going to arrest me and I would meet the same fate as my brother from only a few days earlier.

"They handed me a small box which contained Raymond's belongings and I went on my way home. It was much different when I got home. I saw no neighbors outside and decided that this was going to have to be something I would have to take with me to my grave. I picked up those few newspapers that were still lying in the yard and pulled out what mail I had out of the box and went inside.

"I set everything I had in my hands on the table and then went around the house getting it cleaned up. Occasionally, there would be a knock at the door or someone would try to call me. I simply ignored it. I honestly wasn't in any mood to talk with anybody. Once I had the entire house cleaned it gave me the feeling that everything was getting back to normal. In my mind I would just imagine that Raymond was out on the road again selling something once again from door to door.

That's how I figured I was going to get through all of this, by tricking my mind into believing it.

"That evening I made myself a cup of coffee and got started on the mail. After all it was the first of the month and that meant I needed to get the bills paid. As I was going through each envelope I came to one that made me stop. It was this one," Sarah said holding up a very old and worn envelope addressed to her. "As soon as I saw this I got goose bumps. This is Raymond's writing."

Sarah slowly turned the writing towards her and looked at it. You could almost imagine that same woman sitting at her kitchen table doing the exact same thing all those years ago.

"It was like I was getting a message from Raymond, from beyond the grave," Sarah said still looking at the outside of the envelope. She carefully turned it over in her hand, lifted the seal of the envelope, and ever so carefully, pulled out its contents. Slowly she unfolded the piece of paper that had seen better days and had been taped more than once.

"Sarah, I can't imagine where you are and can only hope and pray that you are safe and out of harm's way. First, I have to apologize to you for not making it back into town in time for Dad's funeral. I honestly wanted to be there. Not to pay respects to him, as you know how I felt about the man, but, to be there for you. And if it weren't for the storms, I would have been, I promise.

"I don't know if you have heard or not, and by the time you get this it will all be over with, but I did plead guilty to killing Andy. The shocking thing is that I really didn't get a trial and the judge has already handed down his sentencing. But no matter what, I don't want you to ever speak a word of this to anyone. Because if you wouldn't have done it, I would have. That's the whole reason why I went to Andy's house that night.

"You see, by the time I got back to town it was fairly late and with all the crap that Beth and I had been going through I really wasn't in the mood to go home. So I decided to stop by Web's and have a drink. Well I spotted Andy up at the bar so I figured I'd go up and have a few with him.

"He seemed pretty shocked and nervous when I sat down beside him. I asked him what was up and he just said he had a lot going on. Knowing him for as long as I had, that usually meant woman problems. I ordered us each a shot and once he downed it that's when he told me.

"He started off by saying that he wouldn't make any of this up because we were best friends, and I agreed. That's when he told me that the chances of Beth probably being at home that night waiting for me were slim to none. As it turned out he had found out that she has been sleeping around with Seth.

"Naturally I got pretty upset over this. Andy could see this and tried to get me to calm down and tried to explain to me that Beth was really no good and that she had been known for sleeping around whenever I was out of town. I asked him how he knew all of this. He looked down at his drink and asked that I didn't get mad at him, but he had been with her.

"It was like a blow to the gut. Here was my best friend telling me that he had been having an affair with my wife, and the fact that I knew you and he were going out made me even more upset. I told him that we through being friends and that he could just forget any relationship with you. As I walked away he begged me to just talk to him, for the two of us to work this out. Right before I left the bar I turned around and yelled at him to watch his back cause he just might end up with a bullet in it. This made the whole bar stop and stare. I really don't know who was in there that night, but there was either some cops or somebody might have called the cops after I left.

"The first thing I did was go straight to the house to see if Beth was there. Just as Andy had said, she wasn't. I don't know how long I stayed there. For a bit, I sat there looking at pictures wondering what I did that was so wrong. How had I been such a bad husband that would make her go to other men? I knew I needed to talk to you, so that's when I went to your house.

"I noticed your car wasn't there and you didn't answer the door so I let myself in. The first thing I noticed was Dad's gun case sitting there in your living room. I walked over to the case looking at the collection of guns in there and finally thought to myself that the worthless son of a bitch finally did something right. I pulled a pistol out and decided to make my way over to Andy's house.

"I really didn't expect him to be home when I got there. Honestly, I figured he would have tried to track you down and talk to you before I had the chance. But I was going to be sitting there in his living room when he walked in and have the last thought be that he regretted ever betraying our friendship.

"As I sit here writing this I wish I had come and talked to you first instead of going to my house. Who knows how everything would have played out. I don't know how you found out about Andy, but I'm sorry that you had to go through that pain. And not for a single moment do I ever regret anything. Remember that Sarah, this is all my doing and you had nothing to do with it.

"There seems to be a lot of secrets going on about the whole affair. I figured if I just pleaded guilty I would get my punishment, serve my time and be on with my life. Sarah, as soon as I said guilty, the damn judge sentenced me to death. I'm hearing in here that the dirty bastard was even having an affair with her. I guess his only way of making sure no one found out about it was to just get rid of me. But you know how rumors are in this place. But don't trust him, don't trust any of them.

"I'm so proud of you and the young woman that you have become. I won't be able to watch out for you as I have in the past, so you make sure to always be strong and trust no one. I always have and I always will love you little sis. Be careful out there. ~Raymond"

Tears were rolling down Sarah's cheeks as she carefully placed the letter back into the tattered envelope. Without saying a single word she slowly began to put all the contents back into the box. Taking an extra few seconds when it came to a picture that had her and Raymond in it.

"Sarah, it's getting late, I think you should get some rest." Brooke said as she slowly stood up from her chair. Sarah didn't make a sound. She continued to place in the box the newspaper clippings, the articles, the picture, the letter, everything. "Kyle and I will be back up early in the morning. I love you, Sarah." Still no response.

"And look Sarah, I'll go through all my law books and figure this whole thing out. There is no need for you to worry about it, I'll take care of you, I promise." Again there was only silence. Josh stood up, took one more look at Sarah, and his heart just broke for her.

Brooke, Josh, and Bobby all began to leave the room. Just before he stepped out, Bobby turned around.

"Grandma Sarah, what do you want me to write in the paper?" Bobby asked with a concerned tone in his voice. He couldn't imagine telling everyone about this deep dark secret Sarah had been holding in all these years.

Sarah slowly raised her head, looked Bobby right in the eyes and said, "I want you to tell them the truth."

Bobby turned and left the room and caught up with Brooke and Josh as they were walking down the hall to the elevator. Josh pushed the down arrow and Brooke fumbled in her purse and pulled out her cell phone. She had a text message from Kyle that said, "Going home." Brooke replied back, "Leaving now."

The down arrow lit up with a ding and the sliding doors opened as all three climbed inside. Josh pushed the L button and the doors in front of them closed. Riding down the few floors the three of them stood there silently. There really was no need for any of them to say anything to each other.

They walked into the parking garage and went their own separate ways to where they had parked. What they didn't realize was as they were all getting into the vehicles a Code Blue was being called in the ICU.

* * * * * * * * *

It had been two days since Sarah had passed away and the next morning was her funeral. Kyle and Brooke were back at the house getting all the last minute details finished up.

The two had barely spoken to each other. Brooke wanted to know what Kyle was thinking, how he was coping with everything that had transpired in these last few days. Kyle simply wanted everything to be over with.

From outside Kyle heard a slight thud and knew that his paper had just landed on his front porch. It was what he had been dreading. Soon, the entire town would find out that his mother was a cold blooded murderer.

He opened the screen door and there, rolled up, he saw his paper. He bent over to pick it up, sat on a wicker chair on his porch, pulled off the rubber band and opened his paper.

The top headline read, "City Imposes Higher Property Tax." Kyle was shocked by this and flipped through the paper seeing if there was any mention whatsoever about his mom. Surely a story of this magnitude would have been front page news. While searching the paper he finally came across the mention of Sarah, on the very last page.

There was a beautifully written obituary that went into great detail about all the numerous things Sarah had done through her life to help make Sumertown the town it was today. It talked about the charitable work she had done, the different organizations she had been a part of, and even included some stories from her past. This was unlike any obituary he had ever read, it was more like reading a eulogy.

Kyle went back into the house and handed the paper to Brooke without saying a word. He went into the kitchen, grabbed the phone book from the drawer and looked up Bobby's number. He answered on the second ring.

"Why didn't you print the story?" Kyle was barely able to get out through the lump in his throat.

"I did print the story."

"No, why didn't you print the story Mom told?"

"People know enough about each other in this town already, whether it's true or not. You know, before I left Grandma Sarah's room I asked what she wanted me to print. She told me the truth, and that's exactly what I did."